THE OUTRIDER

THE OUTRIDER

•

Owen G. Irons

AVALON BOOKS
NEW YORK

Published by Thomas Bouregy & Co., Inc.
160 Madison Avenue, New York, NY 10016

Library of Congress Cataloging-in-Publication Data

Irons, Owen G.
    The outrider / Owen G. Irons.
        p.   cm.
    ISBN-13: 978-0-8034-9831-0 (hardcover: acid-free paper)
    I. Title.
    PS3559.R6098   2007
    813'.54—dc22

                                                    2006101348

PRINTED IN THE UNITED STATES OF AMERICA
ON ACID-FREE PAPER
BY HADDON CRAFTSMEN, BLOOMSBURG, PENNSYLVANIA

This book is dedicated to Lew Slosser—
One of the best of the old-timers

Chapter One

The sun had vanished beyond the far mountains, but its blood-red memory hung in the sky. The wide-spreading oak tree, standing alone on the low knoll, was as black as wrought iron against the crimson sunset. The two marionettes suspended from its heavy branches were dark silhouettes. A soothing breeze moved over the shadowed prairie. It brought no comfort to the two dead men.

They stirred slightly at the ends of their lynch-tethers, nudged by the passing breeze. Dan Featherskill sat his horse watching as the sky began to fade to layers of scarlet and deep purple, the heavier hues pressing the violent red into the darkening earth.

The leggy black horse shifted beneath him and Featherskill placed a hand on its heated neck. He shifted in the saddle, looking behind him. No one was coming, no one would be pursuing him. They had had enough, and they had taken their vengeance.

Featherskill touched the heels of his boots to his horse's flanks and walked it on, following the twilight glow. He didn't glance again at the two hanging men. Their ghosts remained silent as he passed them. It was for the best—he didn't wish to hear them crying out for retribution. He had no killing urge left in him. They would have to be satisfied with the destruction they had wrought themselves and left behind only when the heavy nooses tightened around their throats.

"Featherskill is the man you need," Rory Pitt said. No one paid any attention to him. The group of men stood or sat or paced the office of Colonel Sheen, commander of Fort Riley, Kansas. The colonel was a round-faced man prone to perspire heavily. His white mustache was well groomed, narrow, and his eyes deeply sunk in a fleshy face. He watched the men around him almost with indifference. This had gone on long enough. Every man had spoken his piece and nothing had been decided.

"What I need," John Lovelace, the wagon master insisted loudly, "is for the US Army to do its duty and give my people protection."

"I have addressed that request," Colonel Sheen said. He was fighting back a yawn. Behind him the morning sun was a yellow glare. Dust sifted past the window. On the parade ground a squad of troopers was enduring a punishment drill. The sergeant's booming commands could be heard.

"Why do we have an army stationed out here if they can't even protect civilians!" Lovelace demanded. He was narrow and angular, but when he spoke his voice was like a whip crack.

"Our job is to protect settlers from Indians and outlaws," Sheen said with unsteady patience. "That is why we are here, that is what we do, Mr. Lovelace. Your people have not been threatened by either."

"You know the danger!" Lovelace persisted. He threw his hands in the air as if trying to penetrate the colonel's granite skull was madly frustrating.

Lieutenant Tyler McGee took it upon himself to re-state the Army's position. The younger officer tried to maintain a reasonable tone although the heat was becoming oppressive and the meeting was dragging on into his free time.

"Mr. Lovelace," Lieutenant McGee said patiently. "We know that there have been recent raids on the wagon trains along the trail. When the criminals can be identified and located, the Army will certainly clean the vultures out. However"—he hurried before Lovelace could interrupt him—"as the colonel has pointed out to you and your people, we can hardly be expected to provide a cavalry escort to Colorado!"

"If you don't want to go on to Colorado, don't," Pitt said pragmatically. The little man rose and stretched his arms. Then he walked to the window and spat out a stream of tobacco juice. The colonel didn't even glance at the buckskin-clad scout.

"There is no turning back!" Lovelace said, his face turning redder. He ran his fingers through his thin, dirty-blond hair and wiped the back of his wrist across his fleshy nose. "We have promised these people passage— safe passage—across the plains. They have invested good money in their wagons, their contents and our services."

"I would advise you to hire civilian outriders," the colonel said.

"We would if we could afford them! If we could find any. And how could we trust strangers now? Here. After two of the last trains to leave Fort Riley have been plundered?"

"What they need is Featherskill," Pitt repeated. He returned to his chair and sat down, placing his hat on his head to indicate he wouldn't be remaining long.

"Would you quit muttering about this Featherskill," Lovelace said harshly.

"Is Featherskill in the area, Pitt?" Lieutenant McGee asked.

"In town," Pitt replied, nodding heavily. "I seen him last night. That's what brought him to mind."

"I can see I'm going to receive no help from the Army," Lovelace said in a strangled voice. He put his hat on and glared at the others in the office. His conclusion was exactly what they had been trying to tell him for most of an hour. The man was worried, too worried to listen to words he did not wish to hear.

Colonel Sheen understood the wagon master's fears. There was simply no way he could help Lovelace. His wagon train was composed of eager, young and not-so-young settlers anxious to start new homes in the Western vastness. Most of them were inexperienced; most of them had sold their small holdings and whatever else they might have owned to outfit themselves for the odyssey. They were not Indian fighters. They were homesteaders. Lovelace had taken their money on the strength of his experience and the skills of his men. Few of them were tested warriors either.

Beside these innocents he had promised to guide and protect, Lovelace had taken on an added responsibility, one that promised to be highly profitable for him—if he could reach his destination in Colorado.

He had made an arrangement with a man named Werth, the representative of a large St. Louis-based development company, to lead their heavy commercial wagons laden with sawn lumber, nail kegs, bricks and mortar—

everything necessary to build a small town. Which was exactly what Werth intended to do.

The development company had purchased four sections of prime land near the confluence of the Arkansas River and Big Sandy not far from Pueblo and Fort Lyon. There along the well-traveled road west, near a recent flurry of silver and lead strikes, very close to the cattle trail north, Werth and his company saw the need for a town. They were certain it would prosper if it were built, and that was what they intended to do with the supplies they were hauling.

If those supplies did not get through there would be no town and a dozen good St. Louis businessmen would likely be ruined for life. Lovelace's fortune and his reputation would also be sunk, for he had taken the contract on a contingency basis. If the building supplies did not get through to the town site, he received nothing.

These thoughts were resting heavily on the wagon master's mind, and now as he started toward the door of the colonel's office his small, deep-set eyes held more desperation than fury, though his anger still sparked.

"I thank you, Colonel," Lovelace said on parting. "I hope you will bring the troopers to help us bury the dead if the raiders do strike." Then he stepped out into the orderly room, banging the door behind him.

"Well, that's that, I suppose," Lieutenant McGee said. The colonel lifted his brooding eyes.

"Yes it is, Tyler. Now can we forget about it?"

"It would suit me," McGee answered, but Pitt who had started out the door as well, noticed a suppressed strain in the young officer's voice. He glanced at McGee, nodded to the colonel and, shrugging mentally, went out of the commander's office. It was none of his business, after all.

Pitt passed through the orderly room, nodding to the desk sergeant, went out onto the boardwalk and stood in the shade of the awning, watching as the punishment drill was ended and the transgressors—eight soldiers who had torn up a saloon the night before—were dismissed by the drill sergeant and sent back to the barracks.

"They won't do that again for a while," a voice said, and Pitt turned his head to see a grinning McGee behind him.

"Not until they tangle again with that raw liquor Faragutt sells at the Lion's Den."

Lieutenant McGee nodded rueful agreement. The officer took off his hat and rubbed his hand across his curly hair. It was the color of an old penny, not quite red, not quite brown. McGee was still only twenty-two years of age and his face was unweathered, his eyes clear, his body lean and compactly strong.

Pitt who had lived on the plains and in the mountains for the pasty twenty years, had trouble even recalling his own youth. When the scout removed his hat, the expanding bald spot from which gray, uncombed locks cascaded, was revealed. The two men, civilian and Army officer, were totally unalike but firm friends.

"That was all a waste of time," McGee said, inclining his head toward the colonel's office.

"Well," Pitt said, spitting out a rivulet of tobacco juice, "you can't blame Colonel Sheen. He has to answer to his superiors as well."

"He could have detached a squad of cavalry." The lieutenant's voice lowered to a conspiratorial tone. "At least seen the wagons on their way. What would it have mattered? The Indians are quiet."

"For now. For how long, no one ever knows. The colonel can't strip the garrison."

"No." McGee replaced his hat, leaned against the hitch rail and looked toward the main gate. Lovelace was just now exiting the fort. From around the corner of the gate the two men saw a woman in a pale blue dress and blue bonnet appear. She went to Lovelace, holding out her hands. They could see the wagon master take the young woman's hands, shake his head and glance back toward the headquarters building.

Pitt read the silent dialogue from their distance. Glancing at the young lieutenant, he could see that McGee, too, had understood the conversation in mime. And it struck at the young officer's heart. Lovelace had had to tell his daughter, Ruthanne, that there would be no escort for their wagons as they embarked on the crucial stage of their journey.

McGee was quite in love with Ruthanne.

The wagon train had been at Fort Riley for two weeks, resting their stock, fattening the oxen and mules for the last leg of their journey. Two weeks was plenty of time for a young man and a lively, pretty young woman to meet and talk, go out walking and reach an agreement, Pitt knew.

"I'm going with them, Rory," McGee said tightly. His hands were curled into fists. Pitt glanced at the officer in surprise. "I can't let Ruthanne go out on the prairie without protection."

"Take it easy, Tyler. Getting yourself in trouble won't do any good."

"I won't do anything crazy. I'm going to try again to request a patrol from Sheen. Five or six men—just to see the wagons through to Fort Lyon. There haven't been any raids farther west than that."

"That's halfway across the state."

"I know that, Pitt," McGee said more sharply than he

intended. He was silent for another moment, returning his gaze to the open gate. "I can ask again . . . if Sheen refuses I can request detached duty."

"He's only got two junior officers on post," Pitt pointed out. It was true. Sheen had requested two more young lieutenants, but filling postings in Kansas required the exercise of politics and much patience.

"If it comes down to it," McGee said grimly, "I'll resign my commission! What else can I do?"

Nothing, Pitt thought. When a man was so crazy about a woman and concerned for her safety, he didn't guess there was much else a man could do, even if it meant shipwrecking his own career.

Dan Featherskill was providing the patrons of Heath Faragutt's Lion's Den Saloon with a small sideshow. Other men stood along the chipped bar and sipped at their beer and whisky or played at desultory card games which were interrupted from time to time by sudden angry curses or whoops of success. Featherskill sat alone at a small round table pushed up into the corner of the saloon near the west-facing window.

By his left hand sat a mug of beer, half finished. His right hand rested in a blue enamel tin bowl. Steam rose from the bowl as Featherskill soaked his hand in it, occasionally lifting it from the water to flex his knuckles. From time to time a tiny Chinese woman, no more than four-feet tall, no less than eighty years of age, would emerge from the kitchen in the rear of the building carrying a two-gallon pot of water in her towel-wrapped hands. She would shuffle to Featherskill's table, throw the water in the pan onto the floor and refill it with boiling water. She would then slide one of the row of nickels Featherskill had aligned on the table's surface into her pocket and scuttle away again without either of them speaking a word.

"Well," Featherskill heard a man nearby say to his friends, "that's a dollar-twenty she's made off him." Featherskill smiled without looking that way. He lifted his hand from the steaming water again and worked his fingers. The knuckles were not broken he decided, but they had been swollen to the size of walnuts when he had awakened to the dawn in his hotel room. Buttoning his shirt had been a fumbling exercise in frustration. Jason Devers had possessed a solid jawbone, that was certain. Featherskill did not regret having clubbed the outlaw down, but only that he had been forced to use his gun hand to do it. His shooting skills were going to be off for a long time to come.

He glanced up as a trio of men walked through the batwing doors and stood there blinking, looking around the room. One of them lifted a finger that could only be pointing in his direction and they started solemnly toward Featherskill.

"Dan Featherskill?" one of them inquired as the three men stood around the table where he concentrated on soaking his hand. The speaker was angular, no longer young, but tough-looking. His voice was loud for such a thin man and his lips were compressed with some unhappy thought. At Featherskill's nod the man introduced himself. "My name is Lovelace. I'm wagon master for the party you've no doubt seen camped near the fort."

"Yes." Featherskill's audience waited for more, but the one word was all he uttered.

The second man who spoke to Featherskill was nervous looking, square-built, and wearing a brown twill town suit. He held his hat in his hands, gripping it tightly with large reddish hands. His hair was thin, combed straight back. His blue eyes were watery and anxious. He introduced himself as Adam Werth.

"The large freight wagons you have undoubtedly noticed are owned by my company, Star Development." When Featherskill only nodded in response, Werth went on hurriedly. "There are thousands of dollars worth of building supplies on those wagons, Mr. Featherskill. They *must* get where they are going or the result will be ruinous to us."

"I would imagine so," Featherskill replied. He removed his hand from the pan, examined it and dried it off carefully with a clean towel. "Can't get the swelling down. What I'd give for some ice, though I guess it's too late for that as well by now. I'll just have to wait the soreness out," he said glumly.

"Mind if we sit down, Featherskill?" the third visitor said. He was wide-shouldered, dressed Western-style. His teeth were irregular and yellow and his black eyes somehow wicked. One corner of his narrow mouth was bent downward in an expression Featherskill couldn't read and didn't bother trying to. Featherskill gestured with his right hand and two of the men pulled up chairs. Lovelace, the wagon master remained standing as if he felt he was wasting his time anyway and might decide to leave at any given moment.

The businessman, Werth, was studying Featherskill's face. He was used to sizing up men on the spot, from their language, their faces or inadvertent gestures. It was important in his line of work. He could make nothing of Featherskill.

Dressed casually in black jeans and a rust-red shirt, Featherskill wore half boots and had a Colt revolver on his hip. He was lean, wide in the shoulders. His face was a puzzle to Werth. The man could not be over thirty, but did not seem to be much under. The many tales he had heard about Featherskill had led Werth to expect an older man.

Featherskill's face was high-cheekboned, his nose narrow but not sharp. He wore a dark longish mustache with a touch of wax at either end. His hair was dark, parted in the middle and combed back above the ears where it met medium-long sideburns worn full. His eyes were hazel with flecks of gold that seemed to drift across them. The eyes were unreadable. Was Featherskill amused or simply disinterested in them? Werth could not be sure.

"I hear you cleaned out the Flint Ridge Gang," the man with the yellow teeth said. He sat with his arms crossed on the table, his dark hat tugged low as he watched Featherskill. "Heard you shot two of 'em, strung up two more."

"No, not exactly. The town tried them and hung them."

"Jason Devers was riding with that gang, wasn't he? I'll bet he went down hard."

Featherskill showed no interest in continuing the conversation.

"Please, Sample," Werth said, "we're not here to talk to Featherskill about the past. What we want to know is if he will consider helping us now, in the present. Mr. Featherskill,"—Werth pressed his hands together in an almost prayerlike manner—"will you at least let us lay out our situation and consider taking employment with us?"

Featherskill folded his small towel neatly, examined his hand again and smiled.

"No, I don't think I would care to consider any offer at present. Good day, gentlemen." Then he was on his feet, recovering his hat from a nearby chair. He scraped the remaining nickels from the table and pocketed them. He turned on his heel and walked with quiet, measured steps across the barroom, exiting into the glare of noonday.

"Why, the cocky . . . ," Lovelace said violently, but Featherskill didn't hear him. He was already walking along the boardwalk toward the stable down the block. The black horse was due for a good currying. He paused at the corner to let a pair of freight wagons pass, and before he had stepped from the shade of the building onto the dusty street, the girl with the flashing eyes and golden tresses had caught up with him and, touching his arm lightly, inquired anxiously: "You *are* going with us, then, aren't you? Everything is going to be all right, isn't it? It would just be too unfair, too *dirty* to have to die out on that terrible trail!"

Chapter Two

Featherskill looked down into the girl's concerned eyes. Her fingers continued to pluck lightly at his sleeve. Her lips were parted slightly; a golden tress had slipped from beneath her blue bonnet and the dry breeze drifted it across her forehead. She awaited an answer.

"I'm sorry," Featherskill said, touching the brim of his hat. "I don't believe we've met."

"I know who you are. You're Featherskill!" she said with a breathlessness he didn't understand. Before he could gather a reply another girl appeared. A little one, no more than four or five, dressed in blue with a white bonnet—she held a doll in the crook of her arm, pressing it to her breast. Her eyes were huge, round, anxious. The young woman spoke to her.

"Beth, here he is. This is Mr. Featherskill. Now we won't have to worry any longer."

Featherskill turned as if to glance up the street, unobtrusively removing his sleeve from the girl's clutches. "Miss, I really don't know what you're talking about. If

13

you have troubles, I am sorry about that. But I have not caused them; neither have I come to alleviate them."

The girl's eyes held astonishment. "You're not travelling on with us then?"

"Who is 'us?' Are you with the wagon train, then?"

"Yes, of course," she said with a brief sigh of relief. "If you misunderstood me . . ."

"I didn't."

"You're not going on with us?"

"No. No, I'm not."

"You must!" the young woman insisted. Her little sister—if that was who she was—had approached and now stood looking up at Featherskill with questioning eyes.

"No, you are mistaken," he answered with a small shake of his head. "I mustn't, miss. I have no intention of doing so."

"Please? Is it the money? How much did they offer you?"

"We didn't get to that point." His words were firm, his answers clear, but the woman just wasn't listening, or was unwilling to accept them. She touched his arm again, this time without taking the fabric of his shirt. Her eyes studied his, darting from point to point as if they were following the gold flecks around like fish in a bowl.

"We must talk . . . please, let me have a few words with you?" Featherskill shrugged. There were worse ways to waste his morning than speaking to a pretty young woman.

"All right, but let's find some shade shall we?" he asked, squinting toward the white Kansas sun. "There's a small park a few blocks in that direction."

The woman agreed without speaking. She nearly took his arm, thought better of it and, gripping her sister's hand firmly, she trudged along beside Featherskill, her mouth set with determination, as he crossed the street and walked toward the small park near the creek that flanked the town.

The park had one massive old oak tree circled by white-painted stones, a dozen newly planted maple saplings and six green park benches. The dry wind whipped up the dust and pasted it to the leaves of the trees. There were no birds to be seen or heard.

They sat on a bench facing away from the hot wind and drifting dust. The woman placed her hands between her knees, her eyes briefly far away. The little girl, Beth, stood staring at Featherskill, at his gun as she hugged her doll more tightly.

"You shot sixty-hundred bad men," Beth said solemnly.

"Oh, at least," Featherskill agreed.

Satisfied, Beth went off to play with her doll in the shade of the wide-spreading oak. Featherskill could just smell the creek beyond the row of cottonwoods off to his left, and hear the small gurgling passage of the water.

"I'm Ruthanne Lovelace," the woman beside him said. "I forgot to introduce myself back there."

"Yes, you did. I'm happy to meet you, Miss Ruthanne Lovelace." There was a shadow of amusement in Featherskill's eyes and Ruthanne felt her face blush slightly.

"I suppose I acted like a complete fool. But Father and Mr. Werth seemed certain that all they had to do was offer you a substantial amount of money and you'd hire on . . . they say you have no aversion to money."

"Do they? Who are they, anyone I know?" he asked, automatically looking southward as the crack of a hunter's rifle sounded in the distance.

"No. Don't tease me, please?" Ruthanne said. "I don't

know—someone said it. You know how people talk about someone who's famous . . . whether they know them or not."

"I'm hardly famous," Featherskill said, and his mouth tightened. "If I am, I don't want it to continue."

"I don't even know if you are!" Ruthanne said, laughing without humor. "But they said you were."

"The same people?" he asked, smiling for the first time since she had met him. Ruthanne liked the smile and her response was quick and genuine.

"I must have sounded desperate—back there," she said, lifting her chin to indicate the street. Beth was building a small doll convenience of some sort with twigs and rocks. They both watched the little girl's intent play, her lips moving soundlessly as she concentrated on her project. "But this is a desperate time for us all!"

"It's always hard—moving west," he said, glancing at her and then away again.

"The people with us—most of them—have sold their farms and have nothing but their tools, their teams and a few sacks of seed." She watched him imploringly. Featherskill sympathized, but it was not an unusual situation by any means. "Adam Werth, of course, has more, but what he has on his wagons by way of building supplies is all that he and his company possess."

"Then they're taking a risky gamble as well." But he pointed out, "If they succeed in building that town, they'll make a large profit."

"Yes. My father has a share of their company. They traded it to him for his experience in guiding wagons west." Her eyes dropped and her hands wrung together. "But Father has never come this far west before. Most of

his excursions have been out of St. Jo—that's our home—
onto the Kansas plains. Now these folks intend to travel
into Colorado. Well"—she hesitated sadly—"Father has
never been there and he's frightened."

"Then why . . . ?"

"They offered him a share of their business! Don't you
see? He thought he could make money for all of us: Him,
Beth and me. And we could have a new home we actually
owned—in Colorado—built with the supplies we're
hauling."

"I'm sorry, Ruthanne, someone should have been
aware of the problems involved. You should have hired
outriders for protection."

"There was no money left over! There's no money now.
At first it seemed that it would be an unnecessary safe-
guard. They told Father and Mr. Werth that the Kiowas
had mostly drifted south to Texas, that the Arapahos were
in a peaceful mood. They decided to take the chance."

"Now," she went on in a discouraged tone, "they tell us
that there is a gang of raiders out there who strip passing
wagons clean, drive off the livestock and . . . who knows
what all," she said with a shudder.

"It's true," was all he could say. And that sawn lumber
was worth its weight in gold out on those treeless plains
where most of the settlers still lived in sod houses. If the
raiders knew about the building supplies, the wagon train
would almost certainly be hit. He himself had no intention
of solving these people's problems. As one man, what
could he offer them anyway? Why they had such baseless
faith in his abilities was beyond him. Ruthanne seemed to
read these thoughts in his eyes. She turned her head away
coldly. The little girl, Beth, came running to them on

chubby legs and halted, breathing hard, before Featherskill.

"We've got a big pot of beef stew boiling," the girl said. "And Mrs. Frye's baking some cornbread. Will you be sharing our meal?"

"No," he said with a faint smile. "Thank you anyway, Beth."

"Mr. Featherskill is too busy," Ruthanne said stiffly. She rose abruptly and took her sister's hand. Her pretty blue eyes had gone as cold as stone. "I apologize, Mr. Featherskill, for making such a fool of myself."

He didn't answer. There was no answer he could make. Ruthanne turned sharply and walked across the park, rushing Beth along. The little girl looked back and lifted a small hand to wave good-bye.

Featherskill remained there in silence, his arms sprawled across the back of the bench, his long legs stretched out in front of him, crossed at the ankles. He was sorry for the young lady, for all of them. But they had been foolish in their decisions. Now they would have to find some way out of their predicament, and that did not include his assistance.

The sun had heeled over a little so that it was now in his eyes. Stretching he rose to his feet, tugged down his hat and started back toward his hotel room. He was still battered and bone weary from the events at Flint Ridge. He would nap until sundown, then eat a large dinner. Afterwards, he probably would sit out on the plankwalk in front of the hotel and watch the parade of citizens going about their business. That was enough excitement for him just now. He had a little gold the citizens of Flint Ridge had paid him, enough to last for a good long time in a town where baths and hot meals were always available, and still leave enough left over for the plot of land he planned to settle on, ending his roaring, rowdy, dangerous ways forever.

But a man can stretch out his luck only so thin.

Featherskill walked slowly in the shade cast into the alley. He flexed his right hand, finding it little better, and turned his thoughts to dinner: A thick fried steak and hashed potatoes to start, he decided. The thought of it caused his mouth to water a little.

Then thick shadowy figures burst out of an intersecting alley and draped themselves over Featherskill. One of the attacking men pinned his arms and the other clubbed him down with an ax handle. Pain rioted through his skull and his vision wavered and clouded. He was released to fall to the oily decomposed-granite of the alley. He felt one of them yank his Colt from his holster, felt the hard earth crash against his chin.

Then they started to hurt him with determined ferocity. A boot was slammed into his ribs, driving the air out of his lungs, and four or more blows were driven into his kidneys, sending shocking pain up his spine.

He was kicked again, in the skull, and the crazy flickering lights there expanded and danced wildly. His stomach was knotted with nausea and the ground beneath him swayed wildly in a drunken motion.

One of his assailants straightened up and backed away, panting. Featherskill tried to focus on his face, but could make out nothing except to see that he was bearded and had a full head of long hair.

"That's enough," he grunted to the other man who got to his feet as well. "You mind your own business, get it?" the rough voice demanded of Featherskill. "That wagon train is none of your business!" Then a boot swung back and lashed out again, catching him on the temple, and all of the lights blinked out as the alley floor became a swaying ship's deck, sinking now into a dark and silent sea.

The world was lost in murky gray shadows. Featherskill rolled onto his back and stared upward, causing the pain in his skull to return with drumming ferocity. The sky above the dark forms of the buildings was deep violet. He was grateful for the darkness; the pulsing light of a single star was piercing enough to cause him to wince. He lay there unmoving for long minutes, trying to assemble his thoughts. It was like trying to put together a puzzle with mittened fingers.

He recalled a violent blow to his head—how could he forget it when his skull still rang? There had been two men—or, at least two men. How badly had they broken him up? He flexed his hands, finding the right stiff and sore as usual. At least they had not chosen to stomp on it. Be grateful for small blessings.

He tried to sit up but a sharp pain across his lower back caused him to sag back immediately. His kidneys felt like two glowing embers. His shoulders ached. He touched his ribs and even the tenderest probing caused anguishing pain.

They had done a good job, he thought grimly. But why? They hadn't been trying to kill him or they would have done so. They hadn't robbed him. Why had these two complete strangers . . . ?

Oh, yes. He remembered the man's words now: *That wagon train is none of your business.* But why had someone wanted to beat that into his head when he considered it of no interest in the first place? *Simple,* he thought, *they saw you talking to Ruthanne.*

They. Who? It didn't matter just now. What mattered was getting to his feet, finding his way to the hotel and his soft, soft bed. Groaning, Featherskill rolled over and got to hands and knees. He stayed there for a long minute, panting heavily as if he had just run a race. In front of his eyes was a gleaming object which he finally recognized as his Colt. Struggling, he stretched out shaking fingers, curled them around the butt of the .44 and holstered it. He couldn't find his hat, though.

On his knees now he reached out for the side of the building nearest him, planted the flat of his palm there and tried to rise to his feet. On the second attempt he made it.

Holding his ribs he began making his staggering way along the alley. His knees would not lock and he felt as if he was wading through quicksand. Each breath drew fire into his lungs. His head was hanging as he crept slowly along, leaning one hand against the wall of the building. He peered through his hair which had fallen across his eyes, not wanting to make the extreme effort of trying to brush it away. An orange cat jumped up from underfoot with a yowl and darted away with lightning speed. He smiled crookedly and continued on.

He nearly blacked out twice on his way to the hotel, but struggling on he did manage to reach the outside stairs leading to the second story. Nothing could have encouraged him to drag his battered, bruised and bleeding body through the lobby. He managed to keep on going up the stairs, taking them one at a time, by focusing on the bed, only the soft, soft bed in his room. He had forgotten about the steak dinner by now, and any thought of food would have triggered a bad reaction in his stomach anyway.

Featherskill fumbled the key into the lock and opened the door to his room. The window was open and a cool breeze fluttered the parted curtains. He was unaware of it.

Only the bed mattered and, still wearing boots and gun-belt, he flopped across it waiting for the throbbing in his head to subside, the pain in his body to be swallowed by gentle sleep.

But the pain was too much. There was no sleep that night, only endless pain, and with the dawn light slanting through the window, spreading across the ceiling, he was forced to rise again. He sat on the edge of the bed, head hanging. Finally, he got to his feet and wobbled toward the mirror and wash basin. Peering into the mirror he saw a battered, thin-faced man with dried rivulets of blood streaking his forehead and the corner of his mouth. His face had oil stains and abrasions; his shirt was torn; one eye was badly swollen.

He dipped his hands into the basin and splashed water gently on his face, then took heart, ripped off his shirt and threw it aside, and began seriously scrubbing.

Three wind-buffeted cottonwood trees stood in a clump near the small creek which was a silver thread against the golden mown straw. The couple stood together in the shade of the trees. Ruthanne's eyes went from the gentle eyes of the man with her to the golden ring circling the third finger of her left hand. She lowered her forehead to his shoulder and trembled.

"Are you all right?" Tyler McGee asked. "Are you sorry that we're wed, Ruthie?"

"No! No, Tyler—it's just that it was all so sudden. I expected us to be wed someday, who knew when. In a church, with you in your uniform."

"The uniform is a thing of the past," McGee said firmly.

"I never wanted you to have to decide between me and the Army." She drew back to look up into his eyes.

McGee's coppery hair was neatly parted and slicked down. He still looked uncomfortable in his civilian garments: A red plaid shirt and blue jeans.

"There was no other possible decision. I love you. Ruthie. I did not love the Army."

"Still, it must have cost you. To walk up to Colonel Sheen and resign just like that!"

"I think he knew it was coming. Anyway, the two junior officers he had been expecting arrived yesterday afternoon. He won't miss another second lieutenant. The Army is a vacuum. There are no necessary personnel. Everyone is replaceable. Now I have been replaced and I am glad." He kissed her lightly on the forehead, smiling at his good fortune. In truth, the Army hadn't meant that much to him. He had wanted to come west for the adventure. There hadn't been any great adventures. Only dust and heat and loneliness.

"You'll never be replaceable from now on," Ruthanne told him seriously.

"Thank you." He kissed her once more. It was a wonder—having her for his bride. It had, as she said, happened suddenly. Two weeks they had been together. The thought of losing her had been a waking nightmare. Now he no longer had to worry about that.

Colonel Sheen had not been hearty when McGee tendered his resignation, but he had gone so far as to offer congratulations. Nor had John Lovelace objected strongly. Perhaps his desire for a young, Army-trained outrider balanced the scales in McGee's favor. There were two new men riding with the train, as a matter of fact. Rory Pitt, who was attached to the Army only at his own convenience, had unexpectedly volunteered to come along with McGee, for reasons known only to himself.

"It will be all right now," Ruthanne said with hopeful confidence. "Everything will be all right from here on."

McGee held her closely but did not respond. He was green, perhaps, but not so green as to believe that one more man—or two—would make much of a difference against a band of armed, determined raiders.

"It will be all right," Ruthanne said again, as if to herself. "I'm glad that we won't be needing . . ."

"Him?" McGee said and Ruthanne looked up at her new husband in puzzlement. "Him," McGee repeated, his eyes looking behind her. She turned her head to watch the familiar figure walking his black horse through the cottonwood grove toward the circled wagon train.

"Featherskill?"

"It seems you managed to charm him after all," McGee said. His voice carried distress and an undertone of anger. Ruthanne was shocked at the implied accusation. She could not speak, but only stare at the unconcealed emotions in McGee's eyes. It was her first experience at watching the poison of jealousy rise in a possessive man. She had given McGee no cause for jealousy; she did not understand it. But she knew that it boded ill for the westward journey.

Chapter Three

John Lovelace had been in conference with Emory Frye, the wagon train's wheelwright, and Alvin Gosset, one of Werth's teamsters, concerning an iron tire which refused to set on one of the lumber wagons' huge five-foot-tall wheels when his attention was called to the incoming rider. Straightening, he turned and peered into the morning sunlight then frowned heavily and waited, arms akimbo for the visitor.

Featherskill sat the saddle of his black horse carelessly. He now wore a dark blue shirt and a fawn colored flop hat. As he drew nearer they could see that his face was heavily marked. His cheekbone was purple and green, his eye swollen. When he halted his horse he shifted his position gingerly and winced.

Lovelace approached Featherskill uncertainly. He didn't wish to offend the man; he needed him. Yet, he was uncomfortable having him around. Forcing civility into his tone, he welcomed Featherskill.

"Come to visit, or are you just riding through?"

Lovelace asked in his usual booming voice. Featherskill wondered if the rail-thin wagon master had developed it intentionally as a way of compensating for his physical leanness—or was it just a voice needed for command, for calling out orders down a long line of moving wagons?

"I've come to see you and Mr. Werth. If the offer of a job is still open, I'll take it. We just need to talk about the money and how I do my job."

The mention of payment didn't bother Lovelace, although there was little enough of it left in their kitty. It was the subject of control that needled him. They weren't going to take on a man who planned to just wildcat his way along the trail. Lovelace was in command of this wagon train, and his were the orders a hired man was paid to obey. He managed to keep his feelings out of his response.

"I think Adam's out to the remuda, gathering up his riding pony. Come along, Featherskill—we'll have a talk. Say, yesterday you didn't seem much interested in anything we had to say or offer. What's changed your mind?"

"Some people told me not to come along." Featherskill did not amplify the remark and Lovelace could only shrug and walk on ahead of Featherskill and the black horse he rode toward the remuda beyond the wagons.

Featherskill hadn't expected Lovelace to understand. He didn't expect anyone to understand. Perhaps he didn't comprehend his motives himself. He only knew that he was born a contrary soul. Telling him he could not do something was akin to challenging him to prove that he could. The men in the alley could not have known it but they had achieved the exact opposite of their objective. Featherskill had had no intention of riding with the wagon train. Now he did. They had made a mistake—they had laid down a challenge.

Adam Werth was cinching the saddle on a pretty little blue roan mare when Featherskill and Lovelace found him. The businessman looked up, blinked into the sunlight and appeared momentarily stunned. "Featherskill?"

"He's decided to work for us," Lovelace said. He was facing away from Featherskill so that Werth's changing expression was all that he could see, but Featherskill had the notion that the wagon master had mouthed a few inaudible words to Werth.

The businessman smiled and dusted off his twill jacket. "Certainly. Let's go over to my wagon and consummate the deal, shall we?"

Featherskill remained in the saddle. He wanted to delay the agony of swinging down as long as possible. Werth led his little blue roan and together they went back to the circle of wagons. A few kids scattered at their approach and Featherskill's passing was followed by dark eyes looking out of the lined, weary faces of dirt farmers whose only hope in life lay somewhere on the long trail ahead.

The tailgate of Werth's Conestoga wagon was down. It was shaded by canvas, and so with extreme caution Featherskill swung stiffly down from the saddle and made his way to the platform, hoisting himself up to sit on it, hat tilted back as Werth dug through a small green lockbox, searching for something. Lovelace stood eyeing Featherskill carefully. It was obvious to him that he was beaten up and badly. His expression said clearly, "Are you up to this?"

Featherskill caught the expression and only smiled in

return. Werth turned to Featherskill. "There's a one-page agreement every man with us is required to sign. It only says you will not turn back without permission and that you promise to obey any order given to you by either myself or Mr. Lovelace without question."

Featherskill did not accept the document and pencil that Werth offered. Instead he asked, "How much are you prepared to pay?"

"It's only a formality . . ." Werth said uneasily, still pressing the agreement on Featherskill. When he still refused to sign the document Werth stuffed it back into the green box, exchanged glances with Lovelace and replied to Featherskill's question.

"I can offer you two hundred dollars flat or ten a day."

"I'll take the two hundred. Now, if you don't mind."

The ten dollars a day likely would add up to more money, Featherskill knew, but who was to say the men would have two hundred dollars at the end of this trail? Here, now, Featherskill could deposit the money with the rest of his earnings in the Fort Riley bank and be sure of it.

There was a tight expression on Werth's face as he reached into a small leather purse inside the lockbox. Lovelace's face reflected anger and dismay. Featherskill could see why. The contents of the purse were nearly depleted. Werth handed him the cool solid coins without a word.

Featherskill swung stiffly back onto the saddle of his black. He told them, "I'll be in town if you need me. I've some supplies to buy."

Werth told him, "If you need to store anything, take it to Walt Sample. He's the camp boss—that's him over there by the supply wagon."

He turned to see the man he had met at the saloon, the

big-shouldered westerner with the crooked teeth. He was talking to a shorter, round-faced man. This one wore a thick beard . . . as had one of the assailants in the alley.

"Who's the man with Sample?" Featherskill asked.

"Karl Chambers," Werth said. "Why do you ask?"

"No reason. I just like to know who everyone is." With a nod, he touched the brim of his hat and started on his way.

"That about breaks our bank," Lovelace said as he watched Werth lock the box again and tuck it away.

"There won't be any place along the trail to spend money."

"No," the wagon master agreed dolefully. "I just don't like this, Adam. Two hundred dollars to a man we only know by reputation. We could have hired four or five outriders with that money."

"Yes, but you remember the men we interviewed, John. Trail rats, drunkards and shiftless vagabonds. They were as likely to just take their money and ride out on the plains never to be seen again."

"Featherskill might do the same," Lovelace said, watching the distant figure.

"He might, but as you say. He does have a reputation, and I have to believe he wants to maintain it."

"Still . . ."—Lovelace let his eyes return to Werth's—"who is he? What is he? A gunfighter? A scout? A bounty hunter, perhaps. We don't even know what he is."

"No," the businessman agreed somberly. "We don't. All we can do now, John, is hope that he is the man for the job—because he's the man we hired."

A tall gray mule followed Featherskill along the trail toward Fort Riley for a way. Maybe it was a deserter. Anyone with any brains would leave that wagon train. It was going to be a long dangerous journey guided by fools, left unprotected from scavengers. Featherskill had few ideas on how to protect the homesteaders and Werth's Star Development materials. Perhaps they would be lucky. Featherskill didn't like trusting to luck; he liked having a carefully worked out plan, comrades he could trust, and a clear vision of the objective.

Well, he didn't—and that was that. He would give the men paying him his best; that was all he could do.

After making a deposit in the bank, Featherskill rode up the street beneath the branding-iron sun, pulling up in front of the dry goods store. He sat his horse for a while before swinging his leg up and over and dropping to the ground. The pain and the stiffness would last a few more days. Now every step he took jarred him. A heavy headache still plagued him. His right hand was still swollen and sore. That would go away as well, in time. He didn't like not being in top shape, but that was the hand he had been dealt.

Featherskill went into the dim interior of the dry goods store and gathered a few necessaries. He had picked up a clean shirt and was looking through the jeans, figuring to need another pair after all the time he would be sitting the saddle. A familiar, but long unheard voice hailed him from across the room. Featherskill turned to see Rory Pitt striding toward him. The buckskin-clad scout was carrying a five-pound sack of flour and another of coffee.

"Well, Dan," Pitt said, sticking out a callused hand, "how are you?"

"Well," Featherskill replied, but it was obvious by the way he flinched when Pitt squeezed his hand that he wasn't all that well. Rory glanced down at Featherskill's hand and released it, but said nothing.

"It seems you're traveling," Pitt said, nodding at the

small assortment of trail goods Featherskill had stacked nearby.

"I see you're doing the same."

"Same place? I mean—with the wagon train?"

"It seems so, Rory, though I'm damned if I know why. But you? I thought you had a soft berth with the Army."

"I did. A man gets restless."

"This came on you pretty sudden, didn't it?"

"Yeah," Pitt answered with a slow smile. "I can't let these lost lambs wander out there on the plains by themselves."

"It sounds personal."

"I've a friend—Lieutenant Tyler McGee. *Former* lieutenant, that is. The youngster was a help to me, Dan, when I needed help. I like the kid. Now he's gone and resigned his commission for the sake of a girl. The two of them were at the preacher's this morning, tying the knot. I was there. I'd like to try to keep them alive long enough to share their happiness."

Featherskill nodded silently. He extracted a pair of black jeans from the stack and held them to his waist. "The girl . . . it wasn't Ruthanne Lovelace, was it?"

The scout registered surprise. "Well . . . yes it was, Dan."

"She seems like a fine young lady. Tyler McGee can count himself lucky."

He folded the jeans over his arm and gathered up the rest of his goods. He walked to the counter with Pitt beside him. The salesman bustled over and began toting up everything.

"At least there'll be the two of us now," Pitt said, though his eyes showed little confidence.

"What about Lieutenant McGee?"

"Yeah, you're right, Dan. Three outriders. That's not too bad."

"It's not too good." Featherskill handed the shopkeeper

a ten-dollar gold piece and waited while the man made change. "Isn't there anyone else traveling with the wagons we could use?"

Pitt shook his head regretfully. "They're all sodbusters. Family men who have to be driving their wagons, who know no more about the trail than what Lovelace has shown them on a map."

"Too bad," Featherskill said, accepting his change. They waited for the storekeeper to wrap their goods. "Five or six men would be a help."

"It would. But from what I've heard of the land pirates out there, even if Colonel Sheen had cut loose a squad of cavalrymen to escort us, it still might not have been enough to guarantee we would get through safely."

The two men rode back toward the wagon train together, talking over matters as they went. Featherskill wanted to know what the Army scout knew about the raiders. "I haven't been around, Rory. You—being attached to the Army and all—must have heard something."

"Some. The raiders first got themselves noticed about a year ago when they hit a little party of four wagonloads of sodbusters out toward Hutchinson. Six men rode right up to the party, had them all get down from the wagons— men, women, children—and then they held them at gunpoint while they drove the wagons away. Every single thing those people owned."

"Bound for?"

"Who knows. Thing is, as you know, there's a market for just about anything on the frontier. Folks couldn't bring much with them and now there's no place to buy more goods. Horses, household goods, tools—anything goes for a good price and goes quick, no questions asked."

Featherskill nodded. He could see that. A farmer broke

a shovel handle, he had no choice but to try making one himself. If you had no soap for washing, there was none to be had. Flour, salt, coffee—all were at a premium on the frontier where these simple items were considered luxuries.

"Those people didn't try to fight back?" Featherskill wondered.

"Wasn't time, I guess. By the time they realized what was up, they had six drawn guns pointed at them—and these were family men. A man don't want his wife and kids in the line of fire."

"No. Did the Army go looking for the raiders?"

"They did. But where would you look out there," Pitt asked, waving a hand toward the great expanse to the west. "Most of the merchandise couldn't be identified even if found. The men were masked and couldn't be described well."

Featherskill nodded, and thought of the lost expectations and hopes that had gone along with the stolen goods. Settlers who had sold all, braved all and suffered much only to be robbed by common thieves out on the prairie.

Pitt pointed toward the creek and at Featherskill's nod, the two walked their horses through the scattered shade of the cottonwood trees. They swung down from their horses and let the animals drink as Pitt sat against the trunk of a tree, and Featherskill sat cross-legged before him.

"The next raid was different," Pitt said in a lowered voice. "A twenty-wagon train from St. Jo was attacked at dawn by about two-dozen raiders. There was a gunfight this time, and a big one. Six settlers, including one woman, were killed. A little girl was wounded . . . and they had to take her arm."

"They get any of the raiders?"

"Two of them. Neither dead man was ever identified. Just saddle tramps so far as anyone knew. The raiders got upwards of forty horses, twelve wagons and all their goods. Most of the settlers scattered when the shooting started and hid in a coulee, not willing or able to face the killers. They came back to find the dead and wounded and find themselves ruined a thousand miles from home."

Featherskill meditated silently on the pain the cowardly attacks had visited upon the poor aspiring homesteaders. He did understand a little better Lovelace's fears and frustrations with the Army, not that he could forgive the wagon master his short-sightedness in planning this trek.

"Does anybody have an idea who the leaders are?" Featherskill asked, watching his black horse lift its muzzle from the stream, the sunlight silvering the drops of water on its muzzle as it pricked its ears, listening to a sound only the horse could hear.

"There's been a few suggestions," Pitt said, plucking a blade of grass to chew on. "No proof."

"Who has been accused?"

"Several no-goods and wanted men. No one really knows. But there's one name that's come up time and again. Pitt spat the grass out and leaned forward intently. "I've been putting off telling you as long as possible."

"Telling me what?"

"They say . . ."—Pitt went on hesitantly—"some folks say, that the leader of the raiders is Chalma."

Featherskill stared at Pitt with astonishment. There was denial in his eyes and he verbalized it, "It can't be, Rory. You have the wrong information."

"I didn't say it was so, Dan. I said some people have suggested it."

"He gave me his word, Rory. He would never go back on the outlaw trail."

"I'm not arguing with you," Pitt said with a shrug. They had reached the cottonwood grove and now they rode their horses at a slow pace through the rapidly shifting shadows of the wind-fluttered trees.

"No," Featherskill said more firmly, "Ramon Chalma is not one of the raiders."

Featherskill insisted on his point, because he had to. If he was wrong and Chalma was riding with the raiders then Featherskill had been betrayed and made a fool of by the very man whose life he had saved. It was a bitter feeling, and he brushed it away as unworthy of him.

Deep, deep inside of him a tiny clamor rose briefly: A chorus of angry voices which demanded, that if it was true, if Chalma had gone bad again, then Featherskill must kill the man.

Chapter Four

B y the time they came within view of the wagon train, swung down, and unsaddled their horses to let them graze in the dusty, heated shade beneath the cottonwoods, they had dropped the topic of Ramon Chalma—Featherskill because he refused to consider it, Rory Pitt because he did not want to risk offending Featherskill.

They sat against their saddles on the ground. Pitt lit a stubby pipe and waved out the match, his eyes lifting briefly to a swarm of raucous crows that swooped low over the trees. Then his conversation became more practical.

"Are you sure you're really up to this, Dan?" Pitt asked first through a veil of harsh-smelling tobacco smoke. Featherskill raised an eyebrow curiously. "I've noticed the way you're moving, Dan. You're stiff from head to toe. And your gunhand. Look at that puffed mess of meat and bone. You should have let a doctor look at it."

"There's no doctor here." Featherskill waved a dismissive hand. "It'll be fine. It's gone down a lot already."

"Has it? Looks broke to me." The old scout removed his stained flop hat and rubbed vigorously at his bald spot. Replacing the hat, he continued, "That's something only you can tell. The problem is there's still only the two of us. Three if you count the lieutenant. And he hasn't got a lot of frontier time under his belt. But he'll be willing, Dan. He'll be sure to fight to protect his new bride, you can count on that."

"Or quick to ride off if he thinks fighting might get him killed on his honeymoon?" Featherskill asked, studying the stream of ants at his feet.

"He's not that way," Pitt said protectively. "He's my friend, I know Tyler McGee."

"Ever fought Indians with him? Ridden the hard country?"

"No . . . Dan, don't be hard on the man. He's what we have and we have to have some trust in him."

"All right." Featherskill ran a finger over his pointed mustache. Pitt watched him quietly. He knew Featherskill was used to riding with men he trusted, to having a plan of action prepared, to winning his battles, not going in half-prepared, just hoping for the best. That was what had kept Featherskill alive for this long, made him the admired fighter he was.

Well, you can't have everything always, Pitt was thinking. *This is one of those times when we will just have to struggle through with what we have.*

"When do you figure the raiders will make their try, Dan? I'm thinking it will be as soon as we're well out of sight of the fort and any help, maybe a day or two."

"Could be. Me, I don't expect them to strike until we're farther west."

Pitt considered that. The land here was still featureless, flat plains in all directions. As they neared Colorado the land would rise and twist and become more forested. And the settlers and their escort would be trail-weary, possibly less vigilant, with their thoughts on their goal rather than the possibility of attack.

"We can't outguess them," the scout said, knocking the dottle from his pipe. He carefully toed out the last glowing ember. "How do you want to ride, Dan? I was figuring me on the south, you on the north, the lieutenant . . . *Mr.* McGee, taking the point."

"We can do it that way," Featherskill answered, rising to his feet. He stood looking toward the wagons. The kids were playing within the circle, the adults finishing their packing, strapping down everything as tightly as possible. "I sure wish we had one more man to ride drag. We'll both have to take a turn at that, falling back and then catching up with the train."

"It'll be wearying to the horses."

"I'll ask Lovelace about using a couple of ponies from his remuda. If he can't spare any, we'll have to purchase a few in town."

"It's unlikely they have spares," Pitt said. "Maybe you and me could go into town again this evening and see what we can find in the way of horseflesh."

That was what they agreed to do. After the little talk, Pitt decided to stretch out in the shade for a while and take a nap. Featherskill left him there. Hoisting the packages containing the merchandise they had purchased in town, he began walking toward the supply wagon to store their goods. He was ambushed by a happy Beth Lovelace from behind a wagon.

"You came," the five-year-old said happily, rushing to him. She was wearing her blue dress still, but she had lost her bonnet and there were smudges of dirt on her face as she hugged Featherskill, embarrassing him.

"Well, I'm happy to see you," he said, meaning it, but feeling discomfited by the little girl's enthusiastic welcome. Featherskill was not used to such gestures. He gently removed her arms from his legs.

She looked up with wide, trusting eyes. "I knew you would come. Everybody said we would be safe if you came with us."

Before Featherskill could find an answer, two little boys began calling to her from a distance, and with a bright smile, Beth turned and rushed that way, yelling to the boys to wait for her. He watched, smiling, then he shook his head and plodded on.

Tyler McGee, wearing a plain red shirt above his uniform trousers, strode up beside Featherskill. "Help you with those?" he asked, nodding at the packages Featherskill was carrying.

"Thanks, I got 'em."

"The little girl—you've charmed her," McGee said, and there was a tension in his voice that Featherskill didn't understand.

"Kids generally like me."

"Is she one of the reasons you changed your mind so suddenly?"

"No." Featherskill wanted to explain about the men in the alley, but Tyler went on.

"Or was it her big sister?"

Featherskill stopped, turned and stared coldly into the eyes of McGee. The copper-haired cavalryman's gaze was hard, his eyes smoked with anger. "You're a damn fool," Featherskill said, and he started on again. McGee couldn't be shed so easily.

"I asked you a question, Featherskill!" Then he put a hand on Featherskill's shoulder, turning him. The packages fell away from Featherskill's hold and his left fist arced around in a stunning, surprising hook, landing solidly on McGee's jaw. The former Army officer flew back and landed on the seat of his pants. A small crowd gathered, but they did not come close.

"Don't put your hands on me, Tyler," Featherskill said in a low, deliberate voice. "I don't allow it. As for your question—I answered it. You are a fool. How long have you been married? A day, and you don't trust Ruthanne? You'll never make it as a husband." McGee tried to rise, tried to interrupt, but Featherskill was having neither. He shoved McGee back to the ground with one hand.

"McGee, that girl married *you*, not me. Which of us do you think she wants? Your imagination is going to cause you a world of trouble if you don't get a handle on it and learn to trust your woman."

Featherskill slowly collected his packages as McGee glowered at him. Featherskill told him: "Talk to Rory Pitt sometime this afternoon. He'll tell you what our plans are." Featherskill continued on his way, pausing only to say across his shoulder, "And stay as far away from me as possible. Coming around me can only lead to no good end."

As Featherskill went on his way, men stepped near to help McGee to his feet, but he brushed their assisting hands away, rose, dusted himself off, and stood with his hands on his hips, staring darkly after Featherskill.

Walt Sample was inside the supply wagon, repositioning some goods when Featherskill reached it and placed his own and Rory Pitt's provisions on the tailgate. The camp boss looked around and smiled without pleasure, flashing his crooked yellow teeth. His eyes were black and expressionless. Featherskill saw no trace of the other man, the one with the beard. He had hoped to catch a glimpse of his hands to see if maybe his knuckles were swollen and split from thrashing Dan in the alley.

"You can just leave your stuff there," Sample growled. "I'll put it away." Obviously the big-shouldered man wanted as little to do with Featherskill as possible. That suited him just fine. Things would run a lot more smoothly if everyone with the wagon train just let him alone to do his job.

The sun was low, only its huge yellow rim showing above the bleak horizon, and the air was cool with the gathering of twilight as Featherskill and Pitt returned to Fort Riley. The streets were busy but not crowded. Soldiers congregated in and around Heath Faragutt's Lion's Den Saloon; a few farmers and their families getting a late start home from their shopping drove their wagons toward the outskirts. A knot of four or five cowhands hunkered together on the plankwalk in front of an adobe cantina called Gato Negro. Spanish could be heard within.

Featherskill and Pitt headed toward Joe White's stables, looking for the extra horses they knew they would need on the trail. The picking was slim, but there was little time to scour the countryside for mounts. Featherskill selected a stubby little dun with a tough mustang appearance about it and Pitt chose a leggier sorrel. White stood by with a pencil and paper, trying to encourage them to purchase some lesser stock, but those two horses and a scrubby looking paint pony, which was a good horse in its prime but now was nearing ten years old, were the only horses they bought.

"What do you say we have us a beer before we start back?" Pitt suggested as they sat in White's office, settling the bill. White was smiling with pleasure as he counted out the money. He had gotten the better of them, and they all knew it. Pitt was looking wishfully at the Lion's Den across the street through the greasy window of the stable office. "It's been a dry day, Dan, and there's plenty more of them coming."

"Sure. We'll have a beer if you like. That'll give Joe here time to grain the horses up proper. You'll do that for us, won't you, Joe?"

"Anything for you, Featherskill," White answered cheerfully. Featherskill gave him a look that indicated he meant business. He wanted those ponies to be properly fed tonight.

Leaving the horses as well as their saddle mounts in the stable, the two men crossed the rutted street toward the saloon as the sky turned scarlet and gold with its dying flame. There were many early stars in the purple sky, and a slight breeze had risen from the direction of the creek, bringing the scent of water.

The saloon was loud, crowded, but not rowdy at this hour as Featherskill and Pitt elbowed their way toward the bar. There were soldiers, farmhands, cowboys, townspeople and saddle tramps all pushed together in the close confines. They were all drinking, and with such diverse groups there would be a fight or two before the night was over. It wasn't an unusual occurrence. It was looked upon as part of the night's entertainment. A man without a lump on his head, scarred knuckles or a black eye was looked upon as an aberration.

Pitt and Featherskill found a place at the far end of the bar, nearly in the corner where a poker table was surrounded by five animated players who tossed chips into the pot, slapped cards down roughly, and cursed each other without reason or intended offense.

The beer was barely cool, but it was wet and welcome. Featherskill surveyed the room for familiar faces and then returned his gaze to the card game, watching with casual interest as the winnings changed hands.

Two sodbusters shouldered their way to the bar on the other side of Pitt, and after receiving their mugs of beer began talking. Featherskill paid little attention. One of them said that he had had enough of Kansas and that as soon as he had made enough money to buy a wagon and team he was taking his family back to Indiana.

Then he said, "I'd be sitting pretty now on my forty acres if it hadn't been for Chalma!" Featherskill's head came around to stare at the two. They were of a type, scowling, their faces leathery and weather-lined, although one was ten years older than the other.

It was the older man who had been speaking. The younger one sipped at his beer and replied, "You can't keep dwelling on that, Art."

"The hell I can't! Chalma ruined every chance I had at starting over out here and providing for my family without going back to sharecropping."

Featherskill couldn't restrain his curiosity. "Pardon me," he said, past Pitt, who wore a studiously blank expression. "I've been listening. I take it you were hit by the raiders?"

"That's right," the homesteader said with a lingering scowl. He studied Featherskill, reaching no conclusion about him. "What do you care?"

"I'm riding out with the big train that's leaving tomorrow," Featherskill explained. "What's that you said about Chalma?"

"Heard of him, have you?" the man asked bitterly.

"I have. This was a long time back—Ramon Chalma, do you mean?"

"That's him. Little half-breed killer."

"How do you know it was him?" Featherskill asked. His heart was telling him, *No, the man was wrong. Rory Pitt had been wrong. Chalma was not involved in this!*

"How? Mister, I met Chalma a few years ago too. He looked the same then. Half-breed, isn't he? Half Portuguese or something. Wears his hair long. Always has a necklace made of rawhide and silver conchoes on. Fast with a gun. Quick with a smile; quick to kill."

"You actually saw him with the raiders?" Featherskill asked, still in disbelief.

"I don't lie," the big sodbuster said. He put down his mug and his leathery face fell into a deeper scowl as if he felt he had been challenged. Featherskill smiled and shook his head. This was no night for unnecessary trouble.

"No, sir," Featherskill said calmly. "It's only that I heard he had been killed out in New Mexico." It wasn't true, but it seemed to appease the sodbuster.

"If he was, his ghost is still haunting the plains. It was Chalma, mister, you can take my word for it."

Pitt was watching Featherskill's troubled eyes. He finished his beer and asked Featherskill if he planned to stay for another. "No," Featherskill answered. "I've had enough." He pushed away his still half-full mug and started toward the door, Pitt on his heels.

Outside it had gone to full dark. The town's saloons had come to full life, the plains had gone still and invisible in the night. Featherskill stood for a moment on the boardwalk, looking into the far distances where there was nothing but his thoughts to be seen.

"I tried to tell you, Dan," Pitt said.

Without looking at the scout, Featherskill said, "A lot of people tried to tell me, Rory. I guess I just don't listen real good. Come on, let's collect our horses and get back to camp. This might be the last chance we have for a good night's sleep for a lot of miles."

They rode back to the wagons in silence, watching the waxing moon creep from its daytime hiding place into the skies to gloss the long prairie with its eerie light. Featherskill was lost in a tangle of angry thoughts and Pitt did not disturb him. He simply led the string of fresh horses along and silently thanked his lucky stars that he was not Featherskill.

Featherskill brooded. He fought back the anger and the violent thoughts, but they could not be controlled. When he silenced them like a herd of angry beasts, smothering them with cold desolate thoughts, they would lie silent for a minute or two and then break free and begin their raging clamor once more. They were killing things, Featherskill knew.

And his thoughts were killing thoughts.

The man he had called brother had broken his vows. Now Featherskill must, in turn, find his brother and kill him.

Chapter Five

It was no night for sleeping. There was a heaviness in the air, a terrible, menacing heaviness. Featherskill lay on his back, his blanket loose across him, looking up at the silver moon. He had watched its slow passage through the banks of silver stars. His eyes hadn't closed since he and Pitt had returned to their campsite in the cottonwood grove. The creek made small whispery noises and the nightbirds sang. In the wagon train camp now and then a baby cried. Horses in the remuda nickered and blew. He heard the distant bark of the town dogs once as something stirred them up. He heard all of that, but he was listening only to the angry roar in his heart.

Chalma. *Brother.* Killer.

Chalma had been a charming bright-eyed young man when Laura Featherskill had met him at a grange dance and introduced him to her brother, Dan. There were some around Clovis who did not like Chalma because he was part Indian. It did not bother Dan one way or the other.

Chalma's Portuguese ancestors had first touched Amer-

ican soil over three hundred years earlier when Juan
Cabrillo, a Portuguese explorer sailing under the Spanish
flag, reached California. None of Chalma's family had remained after that voyage, but they had returned fifty years
later, and this time they stayed, becoming fishermen and
farmers.

Chalma's grandfather had married a California Indian, a
Luiseno. (Or not married her, depending on which version
you were given.) The man had been ostracized by the Portuguese community because of that rash act, and he had
taken his Indian wife east, across the California and Ari-
zona deserts to New Mexico, where a tiny settlement of
other Portuguese, settled there by the Conquistador, Anto-
nio de Espejo, in the sixteenth century lingered if it did not
thrive. Many of these people were intermarried with the
Indians, and Chalma's grandfather was welcomed.

Chalma himself grew up on the land, grew bold and tall
and handsome. His background was a blend of near-poverty
and fierce pride. He joined a cattle drive he discovered moving into New Mexico territory from Texas, learned English,
worked hard, and grew reasonably prosperous.

At twenty-five he was confident—or cocky if you
preferred—walking with a swagger, smiling widely with
perfect white teeth.

Laura Featherskill had fallen immediately in love with
the handsome Chalma. Dan had been best man at his
wedding.

The suspicious activity had begun almost at once. Riders from the neighboring ranch had ridden to the Featherskill place looking for stolen horses. Chalma admitted
that he had them, but swore they had been gathered inad-
vertently and he would happily cut them out of the herd
and return them. Not many months later a stagecoach had

been held up and someone had accused Chalma, but Laura had sworn he had been home with her.

Then had come the killing. Two men carting gold ore from their mine to the mill had been held up, one of them shot dead. Again Chalma had been implicated, and Dan had looked into it. Backtracking, he had been able to follow Chalma to a hideout. Chalma admitted that he had been a part of the gang, but swore he had not pulled the trigger. Dan had let him go, angrily telling him to clear out of the territory. Chalma had sworn his innocence, promised Dan that he would go straight. Chalma had no doubt deserved to swing, but Featherskill had let him ride away.

Featherskill had let Chalma go for Laura's sake, but when he eventually told her, his sister's former love had turned to hate. That was when Dan had left the home ranch and begun his own wandering.

"I should have just shot the bastard," Featherskill muttered to the empty sky. Then he rolled over and again tried to sleep. The morning would bring its own set of problems, and these would be real and immediate, not assembled ghosts from his past. He could only hope—*hope*—that he did not meet Chalma, for this time there could be no understanding, no mercy for the killer.

"Dan? First light." Pitt was touching Featherskill's shoulder, and he sat up, rubbing his face. Pitt handed him a tin cup filled with steaming coffee as Featherskill peered out of sleep-heavy eyes at the dull gray of predawn. The first birds were beginning to take flight across the steely sky. It was chilly; steam rose from the ground. In the wagon camp small fires sent spirals of smoke into the sky. Men were leading their teams to the traces.

"I figure we'd best hit the trail before they're ready to

roll," Pitt said. The scout was crouched, his rifle across his knees as he watched Featherskill.

"All right," Featherskill said. "What about the lieutenant?"

"Tyler's already riding, seeing as he's on the point. I saddled your black for you, Dan."

"Good. Thanks for organizing things,"

"It's nothing. I had trouble sleeping," Pitt said with a razor-thin smile which indicated that he knew Featherskill hadn't slept much either, and that he could guess the reason for it.

"From here on it'll only get worse," Featherskill groaned. He levered himself to his feet, his battered muscles complaining still. "Stay alert, Rory—you know as well as I do that just because this is the first day, that doesn't mean the raiders won't try to fox us and hit us."

"I've had that in mind. I'm off now. I'm figuring on patrolling half a mile to the south. Any time you want to schedule a meet?"

"No. There's no telling what might happen to interrupt our schedule. We'll join up at every river crossing to compare notes, help them get the wagons across. Besides that, three shots in the air if it's real trouble."

Pitt nodded and gathered up the reins to his bay horse. Swinging aboard, the buckskin-clad scout nodded, turned his pony and started out, his rifle across the saddlebow. Featherskill finished his coffee, tossed out the dregs and moved stiffly to his black horse. The animal was eyeing him closely, perhaps considering a trick or two. At times the horse became too playful, challenging Featherskill to catch him. Perhaps it sensed his mood on this morning, and knew that play was not going to be tolerated, for the ground-hitched horse held its ground and placidly allowed Featherskill to swing aboard, wincing with the pain the movements caused.

Featherskill sighed, adjusted his hat, glanced moodily at his right hand which was swollen to half again its normal size, and with a sigh rode from the camp as the first color touched the eastern skies and stretched long, crooked shadows out before the black's striding legs.

Hearing hoofbeats behind him Featherskill glanced over his shoulder. It was only that crazy mule again, following along. He would have to inquire as to who it belonged to.

The mule had dropped off the trail by the time the sun was fully risen and the land began to gleam with light. The long fields were golden, the occasional rivulet silver-bright as Featherskill rode north by west. Already he felt sluggish with the sun warm on his back, the land empty and still. He shook himself mentally.

That was the worst part about this sort of job—it was dangerous work yet at the same time there was no relief from the boredom. Nothing but a pacing horse, the long featureless land. He found his course half a mile north of the wagons and stayed it all morning. In the afternoon, as they had planned, he slowed his pace gradually until the wagons—by their dust—were ahead of him. Then Featherskill could study the backtrail, watching for anyone who might be trailing them.

Once he saw a squad of cavalry out on some training maneuver, but they didn't follow for long. And within an hour they had circled back toward Fort Riley, vanishing into the dark band of the horizon.

Featherskill rode on, heeling the black horse to lift its pace a little. At a canter he retraced his own tracks to the west, still studying the surrounding land as well as keep-

ing an eye on his own backtrail. You never knew—
someone might have been watching him and decided to
remove him so that he would have no chance of warning
the wagon train in the event of a raid.

Chalma would think of that. Chalma would first try to
take the outriders—silently so there would be nothing to
plant suspicion in the wagon train as they proceeded on
their westward trek.

He had to stop thinking about Chalma! If it was Ramon, there would be time to settle affairs with him later.
If it was not, he was letting the ghosts haunt him again,
and that was surely a futile exercise.

The sun had passed overhead and was beginning to
heel toward the west when Featherskill turned the black's
head toward the wagons. He caught up with the remuda
and shifted the saddle from the black to the stubby dun he
had purchased. Pausing only to splash some water from a
barrel over his face, he started on again. Now he rode
westward, directly along the wagon train's line of travel.

He passed the wagons, drawing curious glances and
morose stares. Lovelace, sitting on his big gray horse,
lifted a hand as if there was a question he wished to ask,
but Featherskill ignored him and rode on. Fifteen minutes
later he drew even with McGee, riding point. The ex-
cavalryman looked at Featherskill warily, perhaps wondering about Featherskill's intentions, but his thoughts
were only on the job at hand.

"I just wanted to make sure you were up here," Featherskill said.

"What do you take me for, a deserter?"

"No. No, Tyler, I don't think anything of the kind. I just
like to know if my men are all in place. When you were
commanding soldiers, didn't you need to do the same?"

"Yes," McGee admitted grudgingly.

"From time to time I'll be riding up. If we don't watch out for each other, no one will."

"That's sensible," Tyler said, pushing his hat back on the crown of his head. "I'm sorry if I snapped . . . I don't know you very well, Featherskill. I didn't have an idea what you were riding after me for."

"Just what I said."

"Yes, I see that." He hesitated. "About the other business . . . yesterday."

"Forget it, that was yesterday. And as you say, you don't know me very well yet."

He didn't give McGee a chance to respond. Turning the dun's head, Featherskill lifted the stubby little horse into a run which stretched the dun's legs properly. Away from McGee he slowed the dun's pace, patting the willing pony's neck, and resumed his post.

An hour on he spotted a nameless little creek. It was a half mile off, flowing sinuously across the grasslands. The horse would be glad of a chance to drink, and Featherskill and Pitt had agreed that the three outriders would meet at each river crossing to exchange notes and offer any assistance the settlers might need in crossing. Especially at deeper crossings the wagons would need to be floated over, and he doubted many of these pioneers had any experience in performing that hazardous maneuver.

Featherskill rode to the river, observing the long line of wagons, now abreast as the teams were watered. The creek was slow-running, shallow, shaded here by willows and an occasional sycamore. He found Pitt squatting near a low fire where a coffeepot rested on the small rock ring he had built. The scout looked up and nodded as Featherskill swung down, loosened the cinches on the dun, slipped the bit and led it to the creek to drink.

When he returned, Pitt's coffee had boiled and he poured a cup for Featherskill. "Where's Mr. McGee?" Featherskill asked, looking toward the wagons.

"I'll give you a guess."

"I was forgetting he's a married man," Featherskill sipped at the hot, dark coffee. A dragonfly droned past, circled his head and darted away across the water. "You see anything out there?"

"Nothing threatening. It's getting to be settled land, Dan. I passed three, four little farms."

"It'll grow fast in the years to come." Changing the subject, Featherskill said, "At least the creek's shallow." He lifted his chin toward the narrow river.

"Grateful for that," Pitt said. He removed his flop hat, placed it aside and ran a broken piece of comb through his long gray hair. "Here comes company," he said and Featherskill shifted his eyes to see Lovelace walking toward them, followed by Walt Sample, wearing a belted gun and a black hat. Dark whiskers were starting to sprout and shadow the camp boss' chin.

"Did you see anything?" Lovelace asked without preliminaries. "All clear out there?"

"As far as a man can tell," Pitt answered.

"What's that mean?" Sample demanded.

"Just what I said," Pitt said, showing no apparent irritation at the man's manner. "It's like when I was scouting for the Army up in Dakota. They got coulees up there wide enough, deep enough to hide an army on what seems to be flat ground. The Cheyenne and the Sioux used them well."

Lovelace looked suddenly nervous. The gaunt wagon master turned his eyes to Featherskill as if such a possibility was a real threat.

Featherskill said, "There's none in this country, Mr. Lovelace—coulees of that nature, nor Sioux."

His words did little to calm the man. He supposed that Lovelace was going to be fretting until they reached Colorado. He had too much invested in the success of this expedition.

"Crossing the river this evening, are you?" Pitt asked.

Lovelace hesitated, glanced at Sample and said, "Of course! Have to make time, as much as possible."

"It would be good for the teams to have water when they get up in the morning," Featherskill pointed out. Lovelace looked to the sun and shook his head.

"We can't be wasting this much daylight."

Neither of the outriders tried to talk him out of it. It was Lovelace's decision and if he'd rather make a few more dusty miles than have fresh horses and oxen come morning, it was his choice.

"We were just saying, at least the river's shallow," Pitt commented.

"So what?" Sample demanded.

"So the teams won't have any trouble," Featherskill said. "Floating wagons is a bear. Those freight wagons"—he nodded toward the huge lumber wagon with its five-foot wheels—"it's going to take some doing to get them over deep water."

"Y'ever dally a buffalo?" Pitt asked Featherskill. Smiling, the old scout told him, "I was crazy enough to do it when I was young and green."

"What in hell are you two talking about?" Sample

growled. Lovelace shushed his man with a gesture, but he too was curious. Featherskill told him.

"Once those wagons get into current, their natural inclination is to swing their back ends around, downstream. If you let them go, they'll take the team with them. You have to tie rope to the back wheels and keep them from drifting by using horses and lines. A few good cow ponies with a few good cowhands in the saddle can manage it fine if the current's not too strong. That's how the trail drives cross the Brazos, the Red River, when they're moving north."

"I don't see your point," Lovelace said, and he did look perplexed.

Pitt explained, "Well, sir—you don't have any good cowhands or any cow ponies used to rope work. Dan and I was figuring we'd likely be the ones having to do that job for you. And a freight wagon . . ."—he threw the remainder of his coffee into the fire—"that's going to be a little like tying a dally on a buffalo."

"All Rory means," Featherskill explained, "is when we do find deeper water, don't let anyone attempt a crossing unless we're around to help. We've already agreed to meet at every crossing, so there won't be a problem unless someone gets too eager."

"Is there anything you're willing to let us do without consulting you?" Sample asked with stubborn anger.

A dozen remarks came into Featherskill's mind, but he remained silent. There was something bothering Walt Sample like a burr under the saddle, but what? Maybe, Featherskill reflected, that was just the way the man was habitually. Nonetheless, he found himself liking the man less and less with each encounter.

"You might pass that on to Mr. Werth, seeing as they're

his wagons," Featherskill suggested. "His teamsters might be good drivers, but they've seen nothing like these western river crossings in St. Jo."

"I'll tell him," Lovelace said. The set of his jaw seemed determined, but there was something close to apprehension in the wagon master's eyes, as if this situation was one more problem he had not considered before agreeing to guide the settlers to Colorado.

Sample, on the other hand, looked only impatient, indifferent to the lecture. He had probably already been paid, Featherskill guessed, and cared not at all about the safety of the wagons or the outcome of the trek. Or maybe he did care—maybe he would be quite content to see a wagon or two broken up. Featherskill sloughed the thought off. He didn't know Sample well enough to guess at his motives. He only knew him well enough to know that he didn't care for the big man.

Featherskill left the dun standing in the shade, tugging at the buffalo grass that grew there, and walked along the rank of wagons toward the gathering of settlers. Most of them had collected around a pair of fires, eating hastily made biscuits, drinking coffee. He stopped the first man he saw.

"Beg pardon, sir. Can you tell me if anyone's lost a mule? I've had one following me out on the plains."

"Jack or jenny?" the cadaverous stranger inquired.

"Jack. Someone must be missing it. It's been trailing after me since Fort Riley."

The settler stroked his whiskered throat and shook his head. "Not to my recollection. I'll ask around."

"Thanks." Featherskill walked on aimlessly. The sycamores curved gracefully over the creek, scattering their shade. He came upon McGee and Ruthanne in each other's arms and quickly retreated, not wanting to disturb them.

"Did you kill any bad men today?" a small voice asked and Featherskill, smiling, turned to find Beth Lovelace there. The little girl was leaning against a wagon wheel, sucking on a peppermint stick. Beth had smeared its syrupy red juice over her fingers and down her chin.

"Not today, sweetheart. There aren't any around. We're safe as angels."

"I'm glad," Beth said. "I heard some of the men say we'd have to fight them."

"What men?" Featherskill asked, crouching down in front of Beth. He declined an offer to lick her candy cane.

"I dunno. They just said, 'We're sure as Hades goin' to have to shoot our way across the plains.'"

"They said that, did they? Well, Beth, they don't know that. Probably we won't see a single raider all the way to Colorado."

"How 'bout Indians?" she asked, her eyes widening.

"Probably not Indians either." She looked disappointed at that. "Those men were just being prepared in case something was to happen. That's good, but most likely there won't be any trouble."

"You're guaranteeing that, are you?" McGee said from behind Featherskill. He rose to face McGee, who was frowning deeply, Ruthanne on his arm, her lips slightly parted as if she was about to say something she didn't dare.

"There are no guarantees, Tyler," Featherskill said. "And"—he nodded at Beth—"there's no need to frighten people over goblins and such either."

"No," Ruthanne agreed hastily, "there isn't, Tyler."

McGee was standing his ground. "People have to be told the truth to be ready for the worst if it should happen."

"That depends on who the people are," Featherskill said stiffly, his eyes indicating that he meant Beth. It might be worthwhile to remind the men to have their guns ready, but scaring children accomplished nothing. Again, Ruthanne looked as if she might say something, but she decided not to interfere in her young husband's argument. That didn't bode well for the future, Featherskill thought. She ought to be allowed to speak her piece too. Bottling all that up inside for too long would only lead to an angry explosion somewhere along the line.

Neither was that his business. He touched the brim of his hat, smiled at Beth and walked away, feeling the cold eyes of McGee on his spine.

Chapter Six

W hen Featherskill got back to where he had left Pitt, he found a visitor. A gaunt, blond young man was talking with the scout. His clothes were torn, and his flop hat dirty. His face was as pale as a ghost except for his nose which was sunburned and flaking and showed pink flesh underneath. The kid was voraciously eating a tin of crab apples which Featherskill knew came from Pitt's own stores. Near the creek stood a picket-ribbed palomino pony looking as if it had traveled as far as the rider.

Pitt and the stranger's heads both turned at Featherskill's approach. Pitt said, "This here is Billy Cathcart, Dan." The two men shook hands briefly, and Cathcart returned to his tin of crab apples, drinking the syrup from the bottom. "He's ridden down from Dakota—had a tough time of it," Pitt added, stating the obvious.

"What happened?" Featherskill asked.

"I was trapping with my dad and Uncle Duane up along the Milk River," the kid told him. "It was a bad winter. We wasn't prepared at all. Indians took our furs the day be-

59

fore we planned to start back. Dad and Duane got mad, said they was going to get their goods back. Neither one of 'em came back. I waited most of a week and then struck out. A wasted year, but I'm alive."

"Billy says there's a new town a couple of miles ahead, across the river."

"Well," Cathcart corrected as Pitt handed him two sourdough biscuits, "you can call it a town, but it's mostly tents. A couple of soddies. One real log building."

"It wasn't there last year," Featherskill said with certainty.

"Nor six month ago," Pitt commented. "I was with an Army patrol up that way then."

"Oh, it's all new," Cathcart said around a mouthful of dry biscuit. He drank from his canteen. "It just looks as old as the hills. One of them 'throw up what you got and we'll call it a building' places, like a gold rush camp."

Featherskill was silent, watching the silver flow of the river, and the lowering sun which shone through the dark trees on the river's western bank.

"What are you thinking, Dan?" Pitt asked although he knew. Could the ramshackle town be where the raiders were holed up? It might be worth taking a look although it would require Featherskill to leave his post.

Featherskill's eyes met Pitt's in understanding. "I don't expect these raiders to strike at night, Rory."

"Nor me. They ain't Indians, looking to count coup. They ain't burglars. They need daylight to see what they're doing. They'll want the wagons already hitched up when they try to take 'em. No, Dan, they won't strike at night."

"Then perhaps I'll risk taking a look. How far would you guess the town is, Billy?"

"Three, maybe four miles," the kid said, pointing to the

northwest. He corked his canteen and rubbed his belly. "Thanks, Pitt. That should hold me until I can get to Riley."

"Does the town have a name?" Featherskill asked although it seemed unimportant.

"I heard it called Purdy. Pitt, Dan—you men have treated me right, but I believe I'll be going now. I'm going to try to hit Fort Riley tonight." Then, with a nod, he walked to his skinny palomino, tightened the saddle cinch, gathered up the reins and swung aboard. Lifting his hat to them, he rode eastward through the trees.

"You going to ride to Purdy tonight, Dan?"

"Yes. I think I'll switch horses again. Give that old paint pony a try. Rory . . . don't let anyone know where I've gone."

" 'Course not."

"No one. Not even Tyler."

Pitt's face formed a brief scowl. Tyler McGee was his friend from Army days. He wished Featherskill and McGee could be friends as well. "If you say so, Dan, nobody will find out."

"All right. I'll meet you at dawn." Featherskill heaved himself into the dun's saddle. That was still an effort, although the soreness was slowly receding. His side still hurt; he was almost certain that at least one rib was broken. As for his gunhand . . . well, it would get better. It had to get better.

The ten-year-old paint pony had the easiest gait of Featherskill's three mounts. He didn't urge it to greater speed. The horse had its limitations, and Featherskill was in no hurry to reach Purdy. Arriving after dark suited his purposes better.

Just as sundown pulled down the last shade of light and

the moon grew brighter, beginning to dominate the sky, Featherskill spotted in the distance a low clump of structures, no more than a dark wart on the plains, and he guided the paint in that direction.

A few lanterns had been lit as he neared Purdy, helping him note that the town was much as Cathcart had described it, much as he had imagined it. Two large Army bivouac tents neighbored each other. Across what was intended to be a street, stood two soddies and a little adobe which might have been the first structure built. Farther on was the low log building Cathcart had told them about. It had two doors on the front, one on the end and presumably another around back. The windows were notches cut between logs, long and narrow, more fitting to a blockhouse than a saloon, which was what the building obviously was. But then, Featherskill knew, the largest, finest building in any frontier town usually was. More men gathered there, and more money was spent there than anywhere else.

Lantern light gleamed dully in the windows and beamed out the open front doors which were fifteen feet apart. The light formed yellow patches against the dark, churned-up earth, illuminating the dozen or so ponies standing at the hitch rails, and the men with cups and bottles in their hands who clustered near the doors, laughing loudly.

As Featherskill dragged the paint pony past the adobe he could smell Mexican food, and glancing that way he could see through its small, unglazed windows parties of men hunched over platters of food. Dan entered an alley between the saloon and a pair of sod houses and emerged again to find himself in an oak grove. There, behind the rear door of the saloon, a number of other men—six or seven at a rough count—had tied their horses. Dan swung down stiffly and tied the paint horse.

Now what? he wondered. He wanted to look around to see if there were suspicious-appearing collections of items that might have been stolen from the westward-bound settlers—household furniture, for example, that had no business being out here. Also, there should be wagons and oxen if this was indeed an outlaw town. There were no canyons or hills nearby in which such things could be hidden. If they had been taken by people in this town, there should be some sign on them. The problem was how to go snooping around without appearing suspicious.

Featherskill started toward the long log saloon, figuring that was as likely a place to start as any. He glanced up at the moon, nearly half full tonight. He stopped, his eyes on the back entrance of the saloon where one shadowy figure lounged in a tilted-back wooden chair and a second man with a burning cigarette talked to him. He was looking that way, but his mind was traveling in a different direction: Wondering if Ramon Chalma was in town.

Anger flared up at the thought. Featherskill needed to find Chalma, to tell him that he had betrayed Featherskill, to tell Chalma that Laura still lay awake at nights waiting for Chalma to return, cursing the memory of her brother for having driven her husband out of the territory. Laura had not been able to accept the fact that she could have been that wrong about Chalma. So she had to blame Featherskill—*he* had to be the one that was wrong, the one who had run Chalma off.

Featherskill frowned in the darkness and walked on clenching and unclenching his right hand. It still would not function properly! Time, he had told himself, would bring the swelling down, heal it. But now, secretly he wondered if Pitt and others weren't right about it. He wondered if the hand was so badly broken that it would really never be of any use again. Not in his line of work.

Featherskill passed the two men near the back door silently. They glanced incuriously at him and went on with their ribald conversation. The ceiling of the saloon was so low that a taller man than Featherskill would have needed to remove his hat to stand straight. The place was dim, lighted by half a dozen smoky lanterns mounted on wall brackets. It stank of unwashed men, liquor and tobacco. Featherskill eased toward the rough puncheon bar, his eyes darting about the room, searching for that one familiar face he wished to find.

"What'll it be?"

Featherskill turned, startled. In his concentration he hadn't even heard the stocky Swedish bartender step up to him. He ordered a beer, saw the bartender's appraising glance, and returned his attention to the crowded room, noticing the packed-earth floors, the range-dirty clothes and hard, tanned faces. One man wearing an eye patch had challenged another to a game like darts, except they were using bowie knives, throwing them at a mark chalked onto the log wall. Men played at poker, but there were no chips to be seen. Those were city gewgaws and these were wild-country men. The stakes were cash and God help the man who reached for the pot without general agreement. Featherskill saw no bullet holes in the walls, but there was no doubt that the place could explode with gunfire at any time over even a small incident.

"Haven't seen you up here before," the man with the eye patch said, shouldering up to the bar beside Featherskill.

"I haven't been here before. The *town* wasn't here before!"

"No," the stranger chuckled, "it hasn't been here but a couple of months."

"Lot of business for the middle of the prairie," Featherskill said, indicating the crowd. "What are they mostly, cowboys drifting back from railhead?"

The stranger hesitated and then agreed hastily. "Must be. Myself I'm just a saddle tramp. My name's Frank Dilfer."

Featherskill didn't give the stranger his own name. Dilfer continued to eye him thoughtfully, then said, "It sure seems that I know you." He glanced surreptitiously at the front of Featherskill's dark blue shirt, and Featherskill knew what the stranger was doing—looking for holes that might have been caused by a badge's pin.

"There any work to be had around here?" Featherskill asked.

"Not that I know of," Dilfer said, finishing his beer. He caught the bartender's eye and signaled for another.

"Who would know?"

"Beats me," Dilfer said, picking up his new mug, "I'm a stranger here myself."

"Seems like everyone here's a stranger to this town."

"Don't it?" The man eyed Featherskill once more, nodded, and wandered off, working his way through the crowd toward an occupied table across the room not far from the open front door. The man had been sizing him up. Of that, Featherskill was certain. The question was why? And for whom? There could be no answers to those questions. Featherskill was beginning to feel uncomfortable among these aimless men. It seemed that they were just killing time, waiting for a call to action.

Maybe that was exactly what they were doing.

Perhaps he was standing right in the middle of the gang of raiders.

The thought was unnerving, but it was only that—a thought. A gathering of rough men could be found anywhere in the far country where liquor was served and gambling flourished. Still, Featherskill decided to leave. There was nothing to be learned in the saloon without bringing the subject out into the open. And that did not seem like a good thing to do. Chalma was not there—that was all he had wished to discover in the first place.

Outside again, beneath the bright clusters of stars, he stood for a moment, smelling the alcohol-scented saloon breath on him. The half moon was growing smaller as it rose. Tangled moon shadows wove together beneath the oaks.

He decided to take a slow tour of the town perimeter, taking a look for stolen wagons or other signs that this was the raider stronghold. If such a thing could be proven, Fort Riley was still within easy riding range. Colonel Sheen could be notified as soon as morning and clean out the nest of bandits with a company of troopers. But there had to be proof, and an hour later, he had found none.

He hadn't really expected to find anything. Wagons, oxen, horses would have likely been driven on as far as possible from the site of the raids and disposed of, maybe at Bent's Fort, maybe as far as Pueblo, Colorado. But they would have been driven west where all such commodities were scarcer and worth the most. Any horse, ox or mule would be worth plenty at the silver and lead mines they were opening in Colorado these days.

Featherskill slowly circled the town at a distance, searching by moonlight. The paint pony's hoofs whispered in the long grass. Nothing at all. Unless goods were concealed in the forty-foot-long Army tents or one of the outbuildings, there was nothing. Certainly there was no way he could search the tents without being invited, and no one was going to do that.

He had more or less concluded that the town had been built to house the raiders along the westward trail but not to store their loot where the Army might stumble across it. That concluded, he had no proof. Glancing at the stars to read the time by the position of the Dipper, he sighed mentally, turned the paint and slowly began his ride southward, back toward the sleeping wagon train.

Purdy's saloon still echoed with the shouts of its drinking, gambling patrons. The knife-throwing game had been broken up after new players grew menacing with their blades. There had been two fights and one man who had poisoned himself with bad whiskey had been carried away.

In the shadows cast by the building, two men stood, watching the distant rider. The white of the paint pony's flanks showed clearly in the moonlight.

"What do you think?" the man with the eye patch asked.

"I think we have trouble. I don't know what he has in mind, but I don't like it," the shorter man said. This one fingered a collar-type necklace he wore. The silver conchoes picked up some of the scattered moonlight.

"You think it was Featherskill, then?"

"I know damn well it was Featherskill! Don't you think I know what he looks like?" The short, dark man's voice was so tight with anger that his words emerged as strangled, indistinct sounds.

"What do you want to do about it?" the tall man asked.

"Track him down, Frank," Ramon Chalma answered. "Track him down and kill him before he can do us any harm."

* * *

The camp was asleep. The only lantern lit was in the covered wagon occupied by Alvin Gosset and his wife, and that was extinguished as Featherskill walked the paint pony past it. There was a campfire burning very low and Featherskill saw Adam Werth, the teamster, and Walt Sample sitting around it. They looked up but no one spoke.

Reaching the remuda which was being watched by a gap-toothed kid of sixteen or so named Donny Bright, Featherskill swung down and began unfastening the cinches on the paint. Donny was tall and lank and had an agreeable personality. He approached Featherskill.

"How's things out there?"

"Quiet."

"I figured so. My pa figures they won't hit us until we're farther down the trail." Donny removed Featherskill's saddle for him and swept the blanket off. "I'll rub him down for you, Featherskill." The paint pony nudged the young hostler's shoulder.

"He seems to like you," Featherskill said, looking along the string for his black horse.

"And I like him fine," Donny said. "He's a good old boy." He rubbed the paint pony's nose.

"Tell you what. When we reach end of trail, you can have him."

"You mean it?"

"Sure. I don't need three horses. I'm keeping the dun for a second mount. Old paint here is getting up in years, and I ride some long miles."

"Mr. Featherskill . . . I'll treat him like a king, I promise you."

Featherskill began smoothing the blanket on his black horse's back, hoping the old renegade wasn't feeling like playing games tonight. Featherskill still wasn't feeling that frisky, and sleeping at odd hours on the hard ground wasn't going to make matters better. The saddle's weight seemed to have doubled recently. He swung it aboard with creaking joints and aching muscles.

It would get better. It would just take time.

He had been telling himself that a lot lately and it was starting to worry him. Maybe his time as a hunter was nearly at an end. It was a good thing he had purchased those forty wooded acres from Studdard. That was where he had been bound before getting roped into this job. If he hadn't gotten beaten, if he hadn't been so angry, if it hadn't been for one little girl's hopeful eyes . . .

He shook his head and swung stiffly aboard. He nodded to Donny who was still holding the lead to the paint pony, beaming with pleasure, and turned the black northward, circling wide of the camp, riding onto the dark plains, alone, ever alone.

Watching Featherskill ride away, Donny was aglow with happiness. He stroked the paint's muzzle again and looked at its sleek muscles admiringly. Its hide twitched and rippled. Ten years old—well heck, that wasn't old for a good horse like this one! Donny had been promised a horse many times by his parents, but somehow the crops always came up short, or they were always low on ready cash. That's why they were traveling west. Searching for something better.

Donny had been set against the trek. He had been offered a bed by his sister and her husband, but he knew Pa would need him once they reached Colorado. With sadness he had come along, seeing nothing ahead but the long wilderness.

Now at the end of the trail there would be a reward. His own horse! And what a horse. There was no one astir in the camp as Donny looked around, and silently he gave the paint the bit and swung bareback onto it. Just a short ride. A moment's freedom, seeing how it would feel to be the owner of the paint. Donny's eyes darted uneasily from point to point as he rode the paint from the wagon circle. He expected to hear his pa's voice, someone's, calling out to him, asking him what he thought he was up to, but no one spoke in all of the darkness, and the open land spread out before him. There was nothing to be seen, nothing at all but open prairie and he owned it all! He kneed the paint and lifted it into a trot. Then he was riding free and easy, joyously across the wide-flung land.

Frank Dilfer shot him from the horse's back and Donny was dead before he hit the ground.

Chapter Seven

At the crack of the rifle, the settlers fought free of their bedclothes, grabbed weapons, and slipped from their wagons into the confused night camp. Two men had already caught up their horses, and riding bareback through the wagons shouted out, "Up at the point! To the west!"

"What is it, raiders?"

"Where are they! I can't see anything."

"That shot was far off," a calmer voice spoke up.

"Up near the point," someone repeated.

"Oh, no!" The voice belonged to Ruthanne Lovelace. She clutched her nightgown at her throat. Her tangled blond hair tumbled free across her shoulders. "It's Tyler, isn't it? Something's happened to Tyler!" The pitch of her voice creeped upward toward a shriek. "Tyler's the one riding point!"

"It's all right," John Lovelace told his daughter. "We're going up there right now." Walt Sample had arrived on horseback, leading Lovelace's gray gelding.

"I'm going too," Ruthanne said.

71

"No." Lovelace's voice was firm. Ruthanne was not accepting that answer.

"I'll ride up in back of you. Give me a hand, Father."

To avoid further argument, further delay, Lovelace hoisted his daughter up behind him and the men started off toward the point. The plains were faintly illuminated by the half moon which now dangled directly overhead. Ruthanne clung to her father's waist as the horses galloped on.

Ahead they could see that Alvin Gosset and Emory Frye, the first two men to ride out, had dismounted and were crouched over a motionless human form. A paint pony stood nearby, reins hanging.

"It's Featherskill," Ruthanne heard her father call to Sample. "That's his horse."

Guiltily, Ruthanne felt a flood of relief wash over her. She was sorry for Featherskill, but at least it was not her young husband!

Reaching the ambush site, they swung down and approached the body. Frye, hands on his hips, faced them and said, "It's not Featherskill."

"Who then . . . ?"

"Donny Bright," the wheelwright said, and a tremendous curse boomed out as Donny's father heard the news.

"You're crazy, Emory! What would Donny be doing out here? Besides, he hasn't got a horse!"

"Maybe he stole it," Gosset said and was immediately sorry.

"My boy never stole a thing in his life!" Then Bright went to where his boy lay and sagged to his knees.

"Why?" they heard him repeat endlessly.

Tyler McGee, who had not been half a mile ahead when the shot was fired, rode in from his point position, and rushed to Ruthanne who threw herself into his arms, sobbing. The situation was rapidly explained to the ex-Army officer.

"But it *was* Featherskill who was riding the paint!" McGee said. "I saw him myself. Isn't that right, Rory?" Pitt had just arrived from the southern flank. He nodded.

"Dan was riding the paint."

"I don't understand this!" Bright wailed. "Where's Featherskill, then? What's happened?"

"I'm right here," they heard as Featherskill walked his black from out of the night toward the group. Without swinging down he told them, "Someone mistook Donny for me in the darkness. They shot him, meaning the bullet for me."

"You're probably right," Bright said heavily. "What could have made him take your horse? I know he was no thief."

"I was going to give it to him," Featherskill said, looking at the lifeless form of Donny. "I told him when we reached trail's end he could have the paint. He was so excited about it . . . he must have decided to go for a ride to celebrate."

"You gave him the horse?" Bright fumed.

"I told him I would."

"And he got killed because someone mistook him for you?"

"That's the way it looks."

"You lousy bastard," McGee muttered. He tried to pull away from Ruthanne, but she restrained him. "Couldn't you have guessed something like this might happen?"

"No. I couldn't guess the boy would take the paint for a ride."

"He was just a kid!" Bright shouted, clenching his fists.

"You know how impulsive they are. You should have known he'd take it out for a ride, Featherskill. You should have known!"

"I didn't." He fixed his even gaze on Bright's. "How could I know? How could I know that someone was going to come gunning for me tonight?"

"He's right," Lovelace said, stepping up to face Bright and the other angry settlers. This was no time for arguments. "Featherskill couldn't have known. The only man responsible for this is the man who pulled the trigger on Donny."

"And the man who sent Donny out onto the night plains," McGee said, refusing to let go of it.

Featherskill said coldly, "I'll be getting back to my post now, McGee. Isn't that where you belong too? I'd hate to see the raiders break onto us now and kill a few more people. Do you know whose fault *that* would be?"

"Damn you, Featherskill!"

"Get back up on point," he said. Tyler took another step forward, but by then Featherskill had already turned the black's head and was riding off northward, leaving the group of settlers standing in their moon shadows around the body.

Featherskill rode quickly, now and then touching spurs to the surprised black. He was mounted on a fresh pony and his course was straight as an arrow. The sniper would undoubtedly try to circle back, perhaps moving cautiously, an eye on the trail behind him since a man fleeing at full gallop would be calling attention to himself.

Featherskill raced on, leaning low over the withers. He was burning with anger at the killing. And he was angry with himself as well. Despite the reaction he had shown the settlers, he did feel responsible. He *should* have known that Donny would be tempted to ride the paint. He should have cautioned him. He *should* have known that after putting in an appearance in Purdy, there was a chance that someone might be following him. Now Donny was dead, and a part of that was Featherskill's fault even though he had made his gesture only generously.

Ahead—was that a horseman? Featherskill rose in the stirrups briefly. He could not be sure and so he hurried the black along. If it was a horseman, was it the sniper? Anybody could be riding the prairie at night, though not many sensible men would be unless they were on important business.

The black under Featherskill was built for speed and now it had shaken off its occasional contrary lethargy and put its heart into the race. Featherskill thought he could see lanterns from Purdy now in the distance, glowing like fireflies. And he again caught sight of a fleeing man.

The rider ahead paused, hesitated, and put the heels to the horse he rode. Now Featherskill had the advantage. He had the faster horse and his black had traveled only half the distance that the sniper's mount had. The fugitive began whipping his pony with the ends of his reins, Featherskill saw, but to little avail. The roan—Featherskill could tell by moonlight that it was a roan—was tiring and had no more speed to offer.

He would never outrace Featherskill to Purdy, and the outlaw seemed to realize it at the same time. He wheeled his mount and slid his rifle from the saddle boot, shouldered it and aimed at the onrushing Featherskill.

A bullet zipped past his head and he saw flame blossom form the muzzle of the rifle. The man was a marksman. There can be no tougher shot than hitting a man on a moving horse from the unsteady platform of another horse's back. Featherskill raced on heedlessly.

A second shot winged off into the distance. Featherskill saw the man's face, mouth gaping in fear, one eye gleaming with starlight. It was Frank Dilfer. Featherskill saw him whip open the lever of his rifle, but before he could click it home again, he was upon him.

He had kicked free of his stirrups, and now, as the black collided with the roan's flanks, Featherskill horsecollared the sniper, the crook of his elbow wrapping abound the outlaw's throat and they tumbled together to the ground as the roan danced away in confusion.

Featherskill landed roughly, jarring his shoulder against the solid earth and he rolled quickly to get on top of Dilfer before the one-eyed man could draw his hand gun or find his bowie knife. Featherskill was on top of the raider, his knees on his shoulder. Dust swirled around them. "Was it Chalma who sent you?" Featherskill demanded, slapping Dilfer hard across the face.

Dilfer's head rolled loosely to one side—and stayed there, his single eye staring up lifelessly. Featherskill's question would not be answered.

"Damn!" Featherskill, wiped back his hair, leaning away from Dilfer's face. The man had landed on his head when driven from the saddle. His neck had snapped on impact. Dilfer was dead.

Featherskill looked skyward, sighed, and stood shakily. He hovered over Dilfer a minute, but nothing was going to change, Dilfer was staying dead.

He searched the sniper's pockets, expecting nothing, finding nothing. Featherskill caught up the roan's reins then, and pondered: Take the roan back with him to show the settlers? Let it return to Purdy with Dilfer over the saddle as a message? Neither option was necessary nor reasonable. Instead he unsaddled the roan, tossing the saddle aside. Then he unbuckled the throat latch and slid the bridle up and over the roan's twitching ears. Slipping the bit he stood with the reins dangling beside his leg and then slapped the roan's haunch, sending it trotting uncertainly out onto the plains.

Featherskill swung heavily onto his saddle. There was nothing more to be done here. He started the black back toward the wagon train. Dawn was not more than a couple of hours away and the black had had a hard run. He would exchange it for the dun again and return to the northern flank when the wagon train started on. Two days were done, and no sign of the raiders. That would not last, he knew. They would come. Chalma would come.

No matter that Dilfer had been unable to answer his question. Featherskill had admitted to himself that the stories he had been hearing were true. Ramon Chalma was riding with these men, very probably was their leader.

For now there was nothing to be done. Featherskill was bone weary. Silence had fallen again over the wagon train. All the world seemed to be sleeping but for him. Here was where they needed fresh outriders to relieve them as they slept. They had none thanks to Lovelace's lack of foresight. He swung stiffly from the horse's back and spread his bedroll on the raw prairie earth. He loosened the cinches from the black and removed the saddle, but he did not set it free to wander. He slipped the bit so it could graze but kept it ground-hitched nearby. If the horse slept, he would sleep. If not, the hours until dawn would pass slowly.

If only he could get an hour or two's sleep to freshen him some. Featherskill yawned, peered at the starry sky through heavy eyelids and was asleep before he knew it, the weariness overwhelming his senses.

The black horse did not fidget for most of the night, but near dawn it became impatient and awakened Featherskill with its pawing at the earth near his bed. He sat up rubbing his head. He glanced up at the black and said, "Satisfied now? You're worse than a child, you know that?"

The black pricked its ears as if by concentrating hard enough it could understand what Featherskill was saying, and watched as he stamped his boots on and rolled his blanket and groundsheet. Standing, he looked in all directions. The wagon train was visible to the south, appearing like a long, low row of children's playing blocks. He could see white smoke rising from three separate cookfires and his stomach rumbled in suggestion.

"Let's go down and get you some water and me some grub."

The black was returned to the remuda. A man Featherskill had not met before, who gave his name as Ray Jordan, took the black as Featherskill hunted up the dun in exchange. The paint pony was missing and he asked about it.

"Rory Pitt took it out about fifteen minutes ago. He told me he don't believe in hexes and he'd ridden dead men's horses before."

Featherskill only nodded. As he skirted the wagon camp he spotted the paint pony and Pitt squatting beside a fire that wouldn't have filled a hat, boiling his coffee. Featherskill swung down and led the dun that way. It felt good to stretch his legs. He was getting saddle stiff. His jeans were salt stiff and he was chafing up a little on his thighs. That being the least of his aches and pains, he gave it no further thought, though he vowed to have a good bath at the next creek they found.

"Mornin', Dan," Pitt greeted him, crouching beside the fire to pour him a cup of coffee.

Featherskill nodded his thanks and sat cross-legged on the ground, finding it was still as hard as it had been the night before. The two outriders sipped their coffee in silence. Pitt handed Featherskill three sourdough biscuits, obviously prepared the day before, and Featherskill accepted them gratefully, thinking he had better break out some of his grub from the supply wagon later on.

Neither man mentioned the events of the night before. There was no sense in revisiting tragedy. After they had finished their spartan meal, however, Pitt did ask, "Did you get him?" He meant, as Featherskill knew, the sniper who killed Donny.

"Yes."

"I figured you would. Anybody I knew?"

"No."

"Too bad," Pitt said, perhaps hoping that Featherskill had gotten Chalma. The scout shook his head then said, "There's another river crossing about ten miles on. A branch of the Smoky Hill. It's not on Lovelace's map, but I know it."

"I might as well stay close," Featherskill said. "Does it run deep?"

"Not normally, unless there's snow melt in the far uplands. They want to follow the Arkansas River along after that, which might or might not be a good idea—anyone would be able to figure we need to stay close to water."

"So we don't have much choice about it."

"No." Pitt got stiffly to his feet and stretched his arms.

"At some point we're going to have to cross that big river, too, Dan." He stood looking not at Featherskill, but far into the distance. "I don't know what in hell I'm doing playing nursemaid for this bunch. Not a brain among all of them."

"I thought you were doing it for Tyler McGee?"

"Well, yes, that's a part of it. Tell you why—I love the young fellow like a son, Dan." Then Pitt smiled. "But he ain't got a brain in his head either."

Pitt's momentary negative thoughts caused Featherskill to reflect again on his own motivations. Not that it mattered now, he decided. He was here. He had hired on, and this was his job, the settlers his responsibility.

"I have to pick up some supplies, Rory. You need anything?"

"No, thanks, Dan. I was over to the supply wagon earlier. Walt Sample condescended to climb up in there and let me have some of my goods," he said sourly.

Featherskill smiled. "Sample and I are good friends too. No matter—so long as he stays out of my way." He had another thought. "Was that bushy-faced friend of his around?"

"Chambers?"

"That's the one. Karl Chambers."

"I didn't see him around. Why?"

"No reason. I think we've met somewhere before. I'd like to ask him about it."

Pitt lifted an eyebrow, but Featherskill had no more to say. He did wonder if he hadn't met Chambers before. Two days ago. In an alley at Fort Riley. Thinking of that led naturally to the original question—who was it that had wanted to warn Featherskill off of this job? Lovelace, Werth, Sample and Chambers? Someone he had never even met, someone who wasn't even traveling with the wagons . . . ? Featherskill knew there was no answer to be found just then. He tightened the twin cinches on his Texas-rigged saddle and climbed into leather, walking the dun slowly through the camp toward the supply wagon.

He did not see McGee or Ruthanne which was probably for the better. The only person he did know that he saw was Bright, and all he got from Donny's father was an understandable scowl.

No one was at the supply wagon, neither Sample nor his bearded helper. Featherskill reflected that after the first day he had not laid eyes on Chambers at all. It was almost as if the man had left the wagon train. Who, he wondered as he clambered stiffly up into the supply wagon's interior, did Sample and Chambers work for? Was it for Lovelace or Werth's company, Star Development? He wasn't sure it mattered, but it made him curious. The more he knew about the workings of things, the more comfortable he felt in an environment.

Featherskill stood gazing around the compactly packed wagon. Sample might be a lot of things, but he was orderly. His own goods must have been packed where they would be easily accessible, in the back of the wagon, he decided, and he started poking around among the trunks, barrels and boxes.

Under a stack of blankets wired into a bale, Featherskill found six brand new Winchester repeaters. Standing there, the blankets lifted, Featherskill was interrupted by a hoarse, familiar voice.

"Find what you were looking for?" Sample asked hotly.

"No. What I found was half a dozen new repeaters."

"And so?" Sample climbed into the wagon, slapped the blankets away and stood there glaring. Featherskill thought the man would have liked to hit him but hadn't the nerve.

"Just wondering," Featherskill said with a meaningless smile which irritated Sample more.

"Do you know how much a new Winchester is worth on the plains?" Sample said, explaining defensively.

"Plenty—to the right people."

"If you mean Indians, go to hell. I don't believe in arming my enemy. I bought them rifles as an investment. I figure to make fifty bucks profit on each when we reach Colorado."

"Smart," Featherskill said, receiving an angry scowl.

"Your goods are in that white box over there. Take what you want and get. This is my area, Featherskill."

He nodded. The man was right—the wagon was Sample's area. Was there anything else in it he claimed? More rifles? Featherskill grabbed a few supplies and descended without another word to Sample. What was the point in it?

He did ask as he hit the ground, "Seen Karl Chambers around anywhere?" but all he got by way of reply was a deepening scowl. Featherskill strode to the dun, stuffed his trail grub into the saddlebags and started on his way, leading the dun until they cleared the camp.

He came upon a man alone, hat at his side, eyes lifted to the far horizon, and stopped to say hello to Adam Werth.

"Oh, hello, Featherskill," the developer said. "Everything all right, I trust."

"So far."

"Yes, that's it, isn't it. So far." Werth smiled grimly and put his hat on. The nervous little man's eyes revealed distant thoughts. "I can't afford to fail, Featherskill."

"I know that."

"The company has a lot invested in this project. If it fails . . . well, Star Development won't exist afterward. It seemed so simple in our boardroom. Build a new town in the West where none exists. From the ground up. The people will come: The miners, the tradespeople, travelers . . . perhaps the railroad."

"Most things seem simpler in concept than reality," Featherskill said. He found himself wondering if Werth was as nervous as he seemed. Was he scanning the horizon for some reason? He decided he was getting overly suspicious. He did want to know one thing: "Who hired Sample and Chambers?" Surprised by the question, the businessman frowned and hesitated before he replied.

"The company. That is to say, I did. Why?"

"That's what I mean, why?" Werth gave him a what-business-is-it-of-yours look but replied civilly.

"We needed help with the supplies, why not take on two men who have some knowledge of the plains?"

"You just ran across them?"

"Featherskill . . ." Werth breathed out sharply in exasperation. "They walked up to me in St. Joseph while we were loading up for the expedition and asked for jobs. I took them on."

Werth pulled his hat on more firmly and lifted a hand in dismissal, indicating that the conversation was at an end. Featherskill watched the nervous little man turn and start back for the wagons. He was still wondering. Of all the businesses and opportunities in St. Jo, these two hard-cases had managed to find Star Development.

Or they had been sent there by someone to hook up with the wagons.

Featherskill swung onto the dun's back. He was definitely getting too suspicious, he thought. No matter where the two men had come from, they would bear watching. They were both shifty and contentious.

It was of no matter at the moment. He shook his head to clear his mind and started the dun out onto the prairie. The sun was low and warm on his back, and grouse rose from the long grass as he went on his way. Here and there were oaks, and in the distance the land could be seen to rise and tilt as they neared Colorado. In a day or two the Rockies would be visible staggered along the Continental Divide. The land would grow more wooded, more convoluted soon. There would be better cover for the raiders.

Featherskill heard cadenced, muffled sounds behind him and he glanced that way. The mule! Still it slogged along after him. Perhaps the animal had gotten loose from some farm near Fort Riley. Perhaps, he thought, it had belonged to someone on one of the earlier wagon trains that had been attacked by the raiders. No one had claimed the lop-eared mule, no one knew anything about it. Featherskill rode on, allowing the mule to follow at a distance. It, at least, still had confidence in him.

That thought led him to think about Lovelace, Bright, Ruthanne and McGee. He had not exactly made friends with them, but that was not what he had been hired to do.

He had been hired, no matter how they chose to phrase it, to kill the raiders before the settlers could be killed, and that was his grim intention. Given the choice between his own survival and those of the prairie wolves, he would not hesitate to shoot to kill. Given the opportunity to rid the world of Ramon Chalma he would rejoice in it.

Chapter Eight

There was no way those faint, scattered sounds belonged in the silence of the willow glade surrounding the pond where the dun watered and Featherskill rested. There was no way that flitting shadow belonged to an animal. Featherskill's hat was tipped over his eyes as he leaned against the trunk of a shaggy willow, watching his horse drink, watching the vague shadowy figure in the brush, listening to the slight sound of a cracking twig as someone moved through the willows. He stretched his arms and let his right hand drop lazily to the butt of his holstered Colt.

Featherskill had come across the little hollow an hour before and was pleasantly surprised to find the pond with clear water. It seemed a good place to rest. He was both hungry and trail weary and the shaded park was welcome. Now he wondered what situation he had blundered into.

It could be a Kiowa. Maybe a kid, the way he blundered his way in the willow brush. The intruder was not clumsy, but that infinite catlike grace a Kiowa warrior possessed was not there. Featherskill squinted toward the last place he had glimpsed the shadowy figure, seeing nothing. Whoever it was he had withdrawn, or was circling.

That caused Featherskill to rise and look behind him, clenching his swollen gun hand. He dropped into a crouch and took three gliding steps into the brush, staying down, listening. Gnats bothered his face and cicadas chirped along the pond's edge. Then he heard, quite definitely, a footstep. He crept ahead, his eyes flickering this way and that.

And when he saw the leg in the brush clearly, he lunged.

His body hit the stranger's at the waist, and as his shoulder drove into flesh, he knew he had been right. And wrong. It was no Kiowa who had been stalking him. And it had been no man. With a sort of embarrassed fierceness he drove the stranger to the ground. She landed on her back, the air rushing out of her.

She had no weapon, but her hands came up formed into striking talons, and broken fingernails raked across his cheek. Hands gripped at his collar and she tried kneeing him. It was futile. She was small and hadn't the strength. Featherskill eased further up on her, his knees pinning her shoulders as she writhed, struggled, pulled and spat.

She had only a half a minute of that in her and she lay back, staring up with submissive anger. "I'm not going to hurt you," Featherskill said. Her reaction was another few seconds of violent struggle and a hateful hiss. She had short dark hair, hacked off as if she had used an Indian's chipped obsidian knife. Her eyes were round and blue and full of fury. She was short, thin from head to toe with a leanness of the type caused by hunger. She had on man's trousers, much too large, cinched up with a rag, and a man's red plaid shirt, sawn off at the elbows.

"I'm going to let you sit up, all right?" Featherskill said. "Don't try to fight me and don't try to run." She shook her head wildly, struggling again. He said more softly, "Promise me or I'm going to keep you pinned there. You won't like it—there's already red ants in your hair."

That seemed to make up her mind more than anything else and she nodded a quick yes. He carefully rolled off her, and she tried to scramble to her feet and run. Expecting it, he grabbed her by the waist of her trousers and tugged her back. She plunked down into a sitting position and sat there, her breath coming in short, angry puffs, her blue eyes sparking.

"Your promise didn't mean much, did it?" he asked. "What do I have to do, tie you up? I just want to ask you a few questions." She stared at him and remained stubbornly silent. "You look as if you need help," he said as gently as he could. He leaned back, squatting on his haunches, arms folded on his knees. "I'd like to help you if I can. You sure don't belong way out here by yourself. Why don't you talk to me."

"You're one of them!" she spat suddenly. She started to rise but changed her mind and sagged back.

"I'm not one of anybody. Who do you mean?"

"*Them,*" she said petulantly. She stared down at the ground and brushed at her hair where the ants had been making their way.

"You don't mean the raiders? The bandits who've been attacking settlers out here?"

"Yes I do!" she said fiercely and she began to speak rapidly, her angry words running past her lips one after the other. "The men who came robbing and killing and ran off with our stock and our wagons, everything we owned, and left us out on the prairie among the Indians without a thing to eat nor water to drink nor hope of returning to civilization."

Featherskill did not reply. He watched the young woman and wondered. The last wagon train out of Riley had departed more than two months ago. Was she telling him that she had survived out here on her own all that time? That would require much luck and a lot of fortitude.

"You been alone all the while?" Featherskill asked. She might have misunderstood his intentions. Her mouth tightened and she scooted a few inches away. "Are there others with you?" Still no answer. Patiently, he told her, "Look, there's a wagon train not a mile south of here, traveling to Colorado. I'm an outrider for the outfit. I can get you back to the wagon and you'll be safe."

"We can't go," she said in a quieter voice. She sighed, ran a hand across her roughly shorn black hair again and shrugged slightly, using only one shoulder.

There were others, then. "Who is with you?"

"There's just me and my father. The others, all of the others . . ." She couldn't go on and he understood. How many people had she seen killed? Friends, maybe family?

"Let me take you to the wagon train," he said. "My name is Dan, by the way. Dan Featherskill."

"Melody," she said, having been prompted. "My name is Melody Singer."

Featherskill smiled. It was a nice name—someone in the Singer family had had a sense of humor. She told him again, "We can't go."

Featherskill shook his head, not understanding. "But, why? You can't stay out here. When the weather gets bad, you haven't a chance. You already look like a sack of bones, Melody. I'm sorry"—catching an evil glance from the girl—"but it's obvious you're not getting enough to eat."

"I set a good rabbit snare," she said stubbornly. Featherskill sighed and got to his feet.

"That's fine," he said, speaking down to her. "I'm glad to hear that, but Melody, you cannot live out here. You won't last long, and you know it"

"I can't go without my father." She looked down at her grubby hands with their broken nails. "And Father can't go. He won't!"

"Let me talk to him, show me where he is. Maybe I can change his mind."

Melody pondered this suggestion while Featherskill wondered what sort of man this Singer was, what would cause him to refuse an offer of assistance when help had finally arrived.

"I suppose I had better let you talk to Father."

"I think so."

He thrust out a hand and after a moment's hesitation, she gripped it with both of her own, and he helped her to her feet. She was even shorter than he had guessed. The top of her head barely reached his chin. She hitched up her sagging oversized trousers, inclined her head and said, "Come on, Dan, I'll show you."

Melody had Featherskill follow her back to the pond where she retrieved her waterbag. "I was filling it up when you surprised me. Her voice, now nearly calm, was appealingly pleasant. They started then through the willow brush which grew head-high along the sandy banks. Melody wove her way along, following a rabbit run which eventually brought them to a low rock bluff, no more than fifteen feet high. On the face of the bluff there was a small opening screened by brush which had been cut and brought there. Behind it was a hollow approximately eight feet wide and twelve deep, not quite five-feet high. In this tiny cave lay a man.

Singer lay on a blanket spread over brush. His head was wrapped in white strips of cloth—a torn petticoat, Featherskill guessed. To one side was another bandage; this one stained brown with dried blood.

"Father?"

The old man's veined hands quivered, his eyes opened. Sunken into a ghostly white skull, they showed little spark. He stared at Featherskill but showed no fear, no excitement. A blankness, deep and somehow disturbing, was all the eyes revealed.

"I've brought this man here. His name is Dan, Dan Featherskill." Melody crouched down beside her father, placing the back of her hand on his gaunt cheek.

"Where . . . ?" the old man said weakly, hoarsely.

"He was at the pond when I went down to get water."

Singer grunted and he made a move as if to sit up, but he couldn't make it, and sagged back.

"I'm with a wagon train," Featherskill told the old man. "It's no more than a mile to the south. I told your daughter that we can catch up with them. They have food; someone can take care of you."

"No!" The voice was surprisingly explosive. After shouting it, Singer closed his eyes as if the effort had exhausted him. He murmured, "We can't go. I can't go."

"If you won't, I won't," Melody said tenderly.

"Why can't you go?" Featherskill asked. When he got no answer, he asked Melody, "What does he mean?"

"There's . . . there's a bullet in his head, Dan. They shot him. That"—she lowered her voice—"and he's frightened for me. He's afraid the raiders are still out there." Her words became a whisper. "He sees them every night—in his dreams."

Featherskill considered this. It was a sort of shell shock, he believed. He had seen men in the war who refused to believe hostilities were over, that they were safe. "May I take a look at the wound?" he asked.

"It's not pretty."

"Not many wounds are."

Melody nodded and nudged her father's shoulder gently, using only the tips of her fingers.

"Father? Dan wants to take a look at your wound. Is that all right? Maybe he can help?" There was no response and Melody looked up at Featherskill helplessly. There was no imagining what sort of pain the old man must be in with a head wound untreated, with no morphine or other numbing medicines available. Melody spread her hands in a helpless gesture. Dan knelt beside the old man and carefully unwound the bandage while Melody watched intently, biting at her lower lip.

What Featherskill found was worse than he had expected. It was a wonder Singer was alive at all. The skull was fractured, and though he could not see it, he knew there was a bullet pressing against the old man's bleeding brain. He avoided Melody's inquiring eyes as long as possible. When he did let his gaze meet hers, there was no need for words. In silent agreement they slipped out of the cave. Melody spoke first.

"You see, Dan, he can't travel even if he was willing."

"No," Featherskill agreed. Any jostling would most

likely kill the man. There was no hope; even if they had one, no surgeon in the world could remove that bullet with confidence. "What about you?"

"I will not leave his side," she said, and it was a vow.

"You can't do anything. If you stay out here, in this country, you'll die as well."

"He is my father, my patient, my friend! Would you leave a friend alone to die out here alone, Dan? If you are, you're not the kind of man I choose to know."

"No, I wouldn't do it. But you . . ."

"Don't say another word. You have already agreed with me. This has to be done! I am his daughter."

Featherskill admired the girl's determination, and her nerve. "All right, then. Look, I have a few edibles in my saddlebags. Let's bring them up. You can at least have a decent meal or two."

"You will need them, won't you?"

Featherskill shrugged, "I can always get more." He added slyly, "Besides, I set a pretty good rabbit snare myself."

Melody almost smiled then. There was brief merriment in her eyes, at least. Her father's moan replaced it with dark sorrow. "I would be most grateful for anything you can spare," she told him formally.

Featherskill was torn. His duty was at the wagon train. Those people were depending on him. Death threatened them on the plains. But here was a woman and a badly injured man who also needed his help, and their need was immediate. Perhaps Melody read this in his eyes. At any rate she told him, "I know there are things you must do, Dan. If you could spare us a few supplies, you will have done all you can."

"How will you ever get out of here?" He turned to gaze down into her eyes. She smiled, very faintly.

"I don't know yet. I shall know when I have done it."

Featherskill couldn't respond. He was amazed at the girl's tranquil courage. Well, mostly tranquil, he thought, remembering how she had fought him like a wildcat. But then she had believed he was a raider, menacing not only her but her father. She was something, Melody Singer, a combination of lady and tiger. It all depended on which door you opened.

He gave her the few supplies he was carrying and then, not wanting to linger in indecision, he swung into the dun's saddle. She stood looking at him, arms wrapped around the meager gifts he had given, and silently watched as he rode out of the basin, not lifting a hand. Not calling out, but only watching.

Featherskill knew he was doing what he must, that he had made the only decision possible, but he was not happy about it. He turned his horse westward, Melody's blue eyes shining in his memory.

The day was dry and the prairie endless and blank. Night was long in coming and his mind remained haunted by thoughts of the girl and her dying father. With the arrival of darkness the silver half moon rose and the plains filled with gray, gloomy goblins. He could see the wagon train now, halted as night had settled, and he started that way. Distantly, a coyote called mournfully and was answered. His eyes narrowed. Coyotes? Perhaps; perhaps not. His nerves were unusually ragged as he entered the camp perimeter and swung down.

He expected to find Pitt camped in his usual position, but the scout was not there. The wagons seemed unusually silent. Featherskill led the dun to the supply wagon. No one was there either. He looked around for Sample, but did not see him. Clambering in he got into his supply box himself, knowing Sample wouldn't like it, not caring much.

Leading the dun, he returned to the remuda to exchange the stubby little horse for his tall black. Ray Jordan, who had been standing eating from a tin plate, nodded to him, mumbled "Just a minute," finished his meal, and took the dun's lead from Featherskill.

"They find the woman?" Jordan asked upon his return. He gave the reins to the black to Featherskill who looked at him in puzzlement. *Melody?* Of course not; that was impossible.

"What woman?" Featherskill asked.

"Mrs. McGee, of course! Ruthanne Lovelace. Who did you think I meant?"

"What's happened?"

Jordan was surprised by the force of his demand. He stuttered a little. "That's right, you wouldn't a known. You wasn't here. That's where everybody is—didn't you notice how quiet the camp is?"

Yes, he had, but Featherskill had given it no significance. "Tell me, what happened."

"Well, no one knows for certain. Just after we drew up for night camp, it seemed that the lady went out walking. It seemed so, though no one saw her leave. But she didn't show up for evening meal, nor could McGee or Mr. Lovelace find her. She weren't in her wagon nor visiting her friends. When it got to be full dark, young Tyler he began to panic and he got a party together. They're searching far and wide."

"She couldn't have gone far."

"Well, sir, she could have. I got a pony missing—the paint. He's gone and so is the lady."

Featherskill's frown deepened. This was unexpected and troubling. McGee must be a wild man by now. And Lovelace. Where in hell could Ruthanne have gone? Had she and McGee had an argument? Perhaps she had decided to leave him. To ride back to Fort Riley. It seemed unlikely. Maybe she and McGee were having early-days friction in their marriage, but the woman hadn't struck Featherskill as being that flighty.

"Is that where Rory Pitt is?"

"Yes, sir. He came in from the south about an hour ago, switched horses and went out. Down the backtrail, he said."

If Ruthanne was heading toward Fort Riley, Pitt would run her down. His Army bay was much swifter than the old paint. Featherskill could think of nothing he could contribute to the search. Still, he felt obliged to join it. He had another thought.

"How many people are out looking for her?"

"Just about all the able-bodied men, Dan. I'd be out myself, except for . . ." Jordan nodded at the horses he cared for, but Featherskill wasn't paying attention.

There are only a handful of armed men in the camp!

It was the perfect time for the raiders to strike. If they knew about it. They couldn't though, could they? Not unless . . . not unless they knew Ruthanne was missing. If they themselves had snatched the woman . . .

"Grab your rifle, Jordan, and keep it close by. There's something terribly wrong here."

"But what do you . . . ?" Jordan started to ask, but Featherskill was already in the saddle on the black horse and riding away. Jordan watched him for a moment then found himself energized by the warning. He started toward his saddle and bedroll where he had left his Winchester.

Featherskill's first thought was to warn the camp, but he had no proof and he didn't want to start a panic among the oldsters, women and kids who remained there. What could this handful of people do to protect themselves against a full-blown raider attack anyway? Very little, unhappily.

Featherskill moved out onto the plains, a round already levered into the chamber of his rifle. He sat the black in the darkness, listening and watching. He heard a coyote howl again and strained toward the sound, trying to discern if it was truly of the four-footed variety, but he could make no determination. He felt isolated, alone and vulnerable.

If there was an attack where would it come from? Probably not the north since he had been in that direction all day and had seen no sign of movement. Not from the rear, since that was the trail to Fort Riley, and men would be pursuing Ruthanne in that direction. McGee had abandoned the point, but that would involve circling ahead of the wagon train's route without being seen.

The south. It had to be coming from the south. Pitt was in from the flank, the way was clear. Featherskill had just started his black southward when the first shots rang out of the night and the raiders appeared like dark ghosts off the plains to swarm over the wagon camp.

Chapter Nine

Featherskill flagged the black horse toward the battle. The wagons were still only dark and tiny forms against the dark prairie, but the rifle fire was brilliant, the sounds of rounds being touched off punctuating the emptiness. Riding nearer, his own rifle in hand, Featherskill could see figures riding and running in this direction and that. The settlers fled out onto open country, their only chance, some turning to fire offhandedly as they ran.

The raiders, on horseback, answered every shot with three of their own. They were already in the camp, hitching horses and oxen to the wagons. There would be no time wasted. A raider picked out Featherskill's onrushing form and fired a shot at him. The man was kneeling near a freight wagon wheel. Featherskill went low across the withers, fired back, missed, and passed directly through the camp toward the far side where the settlers had gone.

He wheeled the black around, halted it and steadied himself to fire. He got off four rounds from the Winchester, caught one man in the leg, and sent another raider tumbling from his saddle. His other shots went wild as his target dove beneath a wagon.

He was in a losing situation. He wanted to join up with the settlers, try to organize them if there were enough people with guns willing to fight—a doubtful proposition. They were set on escaping and he couldn't blame them. They had virtually no chance against the mounted raiders. And there was little time—the first of the wagons was already rolling out.

What of the little girl, what of Beth? He was concerned for all of the settlers, but the thought of the little girl lost and alone, confused, stirred him to heel the horse after the escaping pioneers. Had someone gotten her out of her wagon? Carried her along during the raid?

Maybe Ruthanne had taken her sister with her. No one had mentioned Beth. Perhaps the raiders had kidnapped both females.

There was so much he did not know, so little chance of striking back just now, alone in the darkness. A shot was fired and a bullet sang past his head and Featherskill reined up sharply. The shot had not come from one of the raiders, but from the group of settlers. In the darkness, mounted as he was, he would be mistaken for a raider himself—something he had not considered in the heat of the moment. He tried waving to them, calling out, but only drew another pair of bullets in response.

He wheeled his horse again and rode southward, away from the raiders and the huddled settlers. Perhaps he could circle to the west and do some damage to the escaping bandits. He saw two riders to his left. Were they raiders, or some of the search party returning to aid in the fight?

The moment's hesitation cost him dearly. The first bullet took the black horse in the throat and the animal

started to cartwheel beneath Featherskill. He kicked free
of the stirrups and managed to dive from the saddle before the horse could crush him, but he landed hard enough
to jar the wind from his lungs. His rifle was lost and with
his damaged right hand he reached for his holstered Colt.
He fumbled at it and brought it up too slowly.

Two more shots were fired and Featherskill felt a
sledgehammer blow to his thigh. Fire washed through his
leg and his knee gave. He fell face first to the earth, tried
to rise and was tagged by a second bullet, this one through
his left shoulder. That one did not hurt. The jarring force
of a .44-40 caliber bullet puncturing his flesh and sinew
was as nothing. Featherskill was already passing out.
There was no way the pain could follow him down into the
deep dark vortex which carried him away to insensibility.

There was nothing. In the beginning.

No sound, no feeling, no memory. And then the flaring
pain came with a rush and swept over him like fiery surf,
and Featherskill came alert with a scream of pain. He
tried reflexively to get to his feet, to grab his weapon, to
fight back. Except he could not rise. His weapons were
lost. He could not fight. He was alone, futile and suffering
in the darkness of the cold night.

He managed to sit up, no more. He could see the silver half moon lowering on the far horizon. Nearly down.
He had been out for at least three or four hours, then. No
one had come to find him. Where were the settlers? How
far had he ridden from the camp after seeing them?

Featherskill's head whirled and then began to thud with
awesome heaviness. He could think no more. He sat there
like a lump of clay given a man's form. He passed out.

When he awoke again, the redness in the eastern sky

told him it was nearly dawn. The toothy jaws near at hand withdrew and a skulking coyote backed away, startled by what it had taken as carrion. The coyote circled him twice and slunk away. Featherskill sat up again. He could see his Colt revolver a yard away—a mile distant. He made the extreme effort of retrieving it. It was all that might help him survive.

The attempt sent racking pain through his leg and tore at his left shoulder like fiery fangs. The movement had caused cold perspiration to coat his face. He couldn't see well enough to evaluate his wounds. No matter, he could do nothing to dress them anyway. He would just continue to sit there and slowly bleed to death.

No, damn all! He would not.

The hint of light in the east caused a shadow to cross his eyes and he lifted his pistol to shoot the returning coyote. But it was not the coyote—the silhouetted figure was much too large. And it had one folded ear. It was that crazy mule, standing nearby, looking dumbly at Featherskill. He tried a smile, but found that it hurt his mouth.

"Can't get rid of you, can I?" he mumbled in a voice that was barely distinguishable as human. There was blood in his mouth, and he spat it out. Water. He needed water. Wanted water more than he had ever wanted anything. Lifting his head, he looked around and saw the black horse lying still, dead against the dark earth. It tugged at his heart. That had been a good, faithful, playful animal. It had not deserved such a death. There should be a canteen still looped to the cantle of his saddle. He staggered to his hands and knees and crawled to the dead horse.

This would be the time he thought as he uncorked the canteen and leaned back against the dead horse to drink. This would be the time for Ramon Chalma to find him. Would Chalma mock him, taunt him, or just coldly kill him?

The water was cool; Featherskill's body soaked up the moisture eagerly. The mule stood watching him as the rim of the red sun rose above the horizon and the plains proved to be empty with its illumination. The wagons, of course, were gone. All of the stock as well. Where had the settlers gotten to? Had he ridden that far away from them, or had they fled toward Fort Riley in the darkness? That seemed the most likely although they could be hiding, cowering in some shallow place of concealment. In any case, no one was going to return to check on his well-being. Nor were any of the men who had been searching for Ruthanne apt to find him.

They would either have decided to ride after the stolen wagons or to return with the others to Fort Riley. The second option seemed more likely. They would know they were outnumbered by the raiders and unlikely to achieve much even if they could catch up.

"Won't be any help coming," Featherskill said to the mule, which kept its dull eyes fixed on the strange human. Perhaps it had been following Featherskill, trusting in this man to guide him to a home. If so it had been sadly disappointed. One thought did occur to Featherskill.

"You ever been ridden, mule?"

No answer. Not that it mattered. He had no confidence that he could make it to his feet, let alone catch the mule if it was the least bit balky. Just now he was content where he was. The water had helped a little; holding utterly still kept the flame in his thigh and shoulder from flaring up too violently. He would just sit there, be comfortable and pay no attention to the blood trickling from his body.

He cursed himself mentally, fighting off the lethargic

fog. He could sit there until he was dead and let the coyote and his friends make a fine meal of him. Or wait until Chalma or the Kiowas found him.

Or he could fight his way upright and *try*. Try to clamber aboard the mule, and try to ride far enough that someone might find him and render aid. That seemed as simple a plan as flying to the moon just then, but there was no other way. He slung the strap of the canteen over his shoulder, gritted his teeth and rose, using the body of the dead horse as leverage.

He was upright. All right then! Talk to the mule, try to walk to it. Talk calmly. *Could* he walk? Never know until you try . . .

It took him an eternity to begin, to move on rubbery legs to the stoic mule. The animal's eyes grew wary and it backed away a few steps as he cooed to it, held out a hand as if it held a treat, and mentally begged the mule to stand still.

His hand brushed the animal's neck and he felt its warm flesh shudder at the touch. He continued to talk softly to the animal. He was having trouble staying on his feet and his vision swum crazily. He had hold of the mule's mane now with one hand and the other slipped across the withers to grip the mule's neck. He hadn't the strength for more than one try, and he silently pled with the mule.

"Please, old-timer, give me a chance."

His muscles strained, joints popped, and his wounds tore open again to leak blood, but he somehow managed to lift his body up and over and he found himself atop the mule, clinging to its neck with all of the strength he had left.

What now? He kneed the mule and the animal shook its head, not moving a step. He tried it again and some long ago memory seemed to stir in the animal's brain, for it started forward, moving at a plodding pace, going . . . nowhere.

Moving away from here wasn't enough, he knew, he had to be moving *toward* something. Where could he find help? Any help at all. The only objective that occurred to him was far to the north, and it would be a desperate ride; nevertheless, he decided to try to make it. Once he had the mule pointed in the right direction, he let the animal amble at its own heavy pace, not caring for speed just then.

The day passed in a heated yellow-white glare. Featherskill had to squint to see in the brilliant sunlight. Then there were moments when darkness closed in behind his eyes and the world went dark. It was at these times that he had to lock his hands together around the mule's neck and cling to it before the darkness turned to unconsciousness and he fell off. Falling, he knew, was the same as a death sentence—there was no way in the world he would ever find the strength to mount the ungainly animal again.

He wondered if he was losing consciousness again. The world was slowly growing dark, very dark. But then, glancing to his left, westward, he could see long banners of pink pasted against the sky and he realized the sun was going down. All day he had clung to the mule until he had felt that he was a part of its heated body, that his life, if there was any left, would be continued as a centaur.

Then he felt shade around him. Smelled moisture. Had they made it?

Somehow he had guided the mule back to the pond in the willows where he had met Melody. Perhaps the mule had been there before, he considered. It could have been following when he had ridden the dun there the day before and remembered the source of water.

It didn't matter how he had gotten there, he was there! He lifted himself to look around—and fell from the mule's back. He landed on his damaged shoulder. Pain flooded his arm and leg. He found himself on his back, staring up at the mule's belly, at the dark sky beyond the lace of willow limbs. It seemed a perfectly good place to sleep again.

No, damnit! He prodded himself mentally, sharply. It was no place to sleep. Not in the open, helpless and alone. He had to find the tiny cave again. Find Melody. It wasn't far, he told himself. He just had to . . . getting to his feet again was impossible. As night settled he began to crawl, to drag himself through the willow brush, following the rabbit run toward the cave in the bluff. His hands pawed at the earth, his head swirled, and his body seemed numb except for the pain. He dragged himself on, finding the cave just at full dark.

"I need help," he said. He thought he had called out loudly, but it was only a whisper in the night. Melody could not have heard him. Crawling forward an inch at a time, he reached the cave opening and pulled himself into it.

It was deserted. No one was there. Melody was gone.

He put his head down on his arm and shuddered with total exhaustion. He lifted his eyes once more. The cave was utterly empty. No Mr. Singer, no Melody. The blanket and rough brush bed were gone. There was not a trace of evidence that anyone had ever been in the little cave which now, as the minutes passed, became cold and dark and as silent as a tomb.

Dan!

Featherskill was having a pleasant dream. In the darkness was an angel and she was calling to him. Her face was Melody's face, and her inquiring touch was gentle. It was quite a comfort to find her there at this moment of dying. He had always wished for his very own angel.

"Dan! Are you all right?" Melody said again. She lit a second match as the first one burned down to her fingers. Digging through the small cloth sack she carried, she removed a stub of candle and lit it. She was sure he was alive. When she had first spoken his eyes had flickered open and the corner of his mouth had quivered in a shadow of a smile. Now he was still again and she bent low over him, touching his throat. His pulse throbbed there, not strongly, but evenly. Melody sat back on her heels and tried to think what she should do next.

She could not give him water while he was unconscious. He was wounded, that was certain. His dark blue shirt was stained to deep maroon at the shoulder and down his back. His pantleg was sopped with blood. She did not know what to do first, but she was determined to do something, even if it was wrong.

Otherwise Featherskill would surely die.

Taking her blanket she folded it and formed a pillow for his head. Then she began unbuttoning his shirt. She still had some of the strips she had torn from her petticoat—strips she had used to bandage her father's head. These might be enough to help stanch the blood in his wounds. Bullet holes, she was certain, and slipping his shirt off she saw she had been correct. Diligently she got to work, bandaging the shoulder as tightly as she could, her breath coming in tiny puffs of concentration. Removing his trousers was beyond her, but using his own knife which hung from a sheath at the back of his belt, she managed to cut away the pantleg and examine the wound in his thigh. It seemed to have caught only flesh, although there might have been some ligament damage, she knew. There was nothing to be done about that. At least it seemed to be less dangerous than the shoulder wound which was jagged, flaring out to flaps of skin at the back. Apparently that bullet had touched bone and shattered.

She did what she could which was little enough: Washing the wounds with water, tightly binding them. When she sat back she found to her astonishment that he was watching her. His eyes were feverish, however, and what he said was, "Any water up here?"

"Up here," meant nothing to Melody, but it did to Featherskill. He was speaking to his personal angel, the one riding with him on a fluffy cloud across the clear blue skies.

It was difficult to lift his head from the pillow, so after one try, he gave it up and just opened his eyes to the morning. Sunlight formed a bright archway at the mouth of the cave. A flight of doves passed his vision as he peered out into the brightness of the day.

Where was he? Oh, yes, alone in the little cave. Memory came flooding back. He remembered riding the mule, clawing his way up here. And then? His shoulder felt strange, tightly bound. Running fingers across his chest, he discovered that he was shirtless. What . . . ?

"Good morning, Dan," Melody said cheerfully.

She stood there in the new sunlight—small, smiling and welcoming. Featherskill thought no more about his angel.

"I thought you were gone," he mumbled. His mouth had filled with blood again, he found. Melody unshouldered her waterbag and knelt by his side to give him a drink.

"I was gone. I was going to walk out of this country— as soon as I decided which way to go. I had already begun when I heard the most awful sound on God's earth." Dan looked at her curiously and she laughed. "A mule! I heard a mule braying. Like a big raucous bellow. A foghorn of a sound. I came back and crept down to the pond, and there was this mule looking directly at me.

"At first I thought, 'What luck! Maybe I can ride this mule out of here.' Then I started to think, and I decided it must belong to someone. Someone who had ridden in on it. Someone who knew about this place . . .

"And you were the only one I could think of who knew about the pond. I came up to the cave—and there you were. I thought you were dead."

"I thought I was too."

"I don't think you were far from it." Melody frowned. "I don't think you're that far from it now."

"I'm fine."

"Are you? Come on, then. Let's be on our way out of here." She teased him unmercifully. "Can't do it? No matter. Just get to your feet—we'll go down to the pond so that you can wash off. No? Oh, well, sit up Dan and I'll find something for you to eat."

"All right, you win. I'm far from all right."

"But you will get better." There was determination in her voice. "I will see to that."

"Melody"—Featherskill's voice dropped as he studied the woman in those hitched up pants and oversized, cutoff shirt—"your father has . . . ?"

"Just after you left," she said with a distant smile. "There was no pain at the end, at least I think there wasn't. I buried him by caving in a sandy bank over him. Then I was the last one left in my family and nobody knew I was alive. And now"—her smile broadened, showing small white teeth—"here you are back again."

"Another patient for you," Featherskill said unhappily.

"Maybe I am destined to be a nurse."

"How do the wounds look?"

She described them, telling him that the damaged thigh looked as if it would heal cleanly. About his other wound she was not sure. His shoulder blade had suffered some damage. His shoulder, at the least, would remain stiff for a very, very long time.

He had survived, that was all that mattered for the moment. They lived on roots and bulbs and snared rabbits. There were small fish in the pond, but Melody was unable to catch them or design a net. One day she did manage to bring down a deer with his handgun and she dressed it, cut the meat into strips to smoke and they had an abundant supply of venison jerky. The woman never complained, never bemoaned her fate. Featherskill liked to watch her fuss about and when she was gone he missed her terribly.

His body began to put itself together slowly. The earlier injuries, those he had gotten in the beating he had taken in the alley, became insignificant and then passed into memory. Within a week his leg was well enough for him to hobble around the cave with the aid of a rough cane Melody had cut for him. He would not be walking long or climbing for quite a while, though.

His shoulder was a different matter. Something had been shattered up there and it was painful to move. He could feel bone grating against bone. They tried to immobilize it with bandages; it did not seem to want to heal properly.

Nor did his gun hand.

Everyone had been right. He hadn't simply bruised his knuckles on Jason Devers' jaw while capturing the killer; he had shattered his hand. It would always be stiff, always painful. For a while, with idle time on his hands, he tried to learn to draw and fire with his left hand, reversing his holster. It was a futile exercise—the pistol just did not feel right. And his injured left shoulder complained with each attempted draw. He had to face it, his days as a fast-draw artist were in the past.

Which led his thoughts to what was to become of him now. His line of work had apparently come to a dead end. His reputation would already be in shambles after news of the raid on the Star Development wagon train was passed around. He had completely failed to protect the shipment and the settlers. Not only that, people would begin to wonder about him. Where was he? Had he just abandoned the wagons to the raiders? Maybe Ramon Chalma had scared him off—or worse, bought him off.

"Why would you want to fight for money anyway?" Melody asked him one night as they sat near to a tiny campfire, watching the starry skies. "This," she said, indicating his wounds, "is all it can lead to. That and worse."

"I know. It was just always a thing I did well. When I was young I was fearless, when I got a little older experience got me by. Anything seemed better than settling down."

"But you told me that you have a little ranch, forty acres that you intended to settle down on."

Featherskill smiled. "Yes, Melody. It's so. What I didn't tell you is that I've been planning on settling down on that land for ten years now. I always intended to go there after one more job. Well," he shrugged, "there was always one more and then one more."

"But now!" Her eyes were bright and curious. "Surely that was your last job, Dan." She wiped back a strand of hair from her brow. The fire touched a bit of pitch and tiny sparks shot up. Her words seemed to be an important question to her. He was long in answering.

"So it seems," Featherskill said, using both of his hands

to shift his wounded leg a little. "But it is not completed, Melody." He lifted his eyes to hers, searching for understanding. "I haven't finished what I set out to do, what I was hired to do."

"You were hired to guard the wagon train."

"Yes. But there is more to it. People were harmed—simple people who only wanted to try to carve out a new life for themselves. People were killed. Someone profited from that. I can't let them get away with their crime."

Melody hesitated. They had spoken before, many times. In the night when the hours passed slowly, when his pain did not allow him to sleep well.

"Is it Chalma, you really mean, Dan? Is it him you feel you must settle accounts with?"

"Yes. And whoever was working with him."

"Who do you mean?"

"Someone sold out the wagon train. How could Chalma's men know that Ruthanne was riding out? How could they know to kidnap her. By chance? It seems unlikely. The men were led away, the attack synchronized with the search for the missing woman."

"You can't be sure," she said. Featherskill did not answer. She asked, "Who then Dan? Who and why?"

"Either Adam Werth or Lovelace, or the two of them in concert. There was thousands of dollars in building supplies on that wagon train. They might offer to turn over all the wagons, all the stock and goods the settlers carried in exchange for their split—the lumber and bricks and mortar and nails. Chalma is hardly going to put down roots enough to build himself a town! Or stay long in one. He's a prairie wolf, not a house dog."

"Why those two, Werth and Lovelace?"

"I don't know. It seems logical. They would have

needed help—Sample and Chambers, for instance, maybe more men. I'm almost sure it was Sample and Chambers who beat me up to try to prevent me from riding with the wagon train in the first place."

Melody had heard about all of these men before; she had listened more than once to Featherskill's theories. She wanted to find flaws in his reasoning, she wanted to see where his thinking was wrong. For one reason—she did not want him returning to the battle which he could not win. He could not beat Chalma. Not now, not as he was. It would have been a monumental task when he was healthy and whole. Now it was utter folly to consider it.

"Leave it," she said very quietly. He seemed not to hear her. Or she was simply being ignored again. He did not seem to understand what she was thinking. Perhaps she was foolish, but sheltered in the back of her mind was a small ranch in northern Kansas.

And Dan Featherskill.

The fire burned to embers and then was extinguished by the night, and they rose to return to the cave and get ready for bed, the conversation ended. But not Melody Singer's lingering hopes. She lay awake for a long while afterward, thinking. *If he will not give up the fight, at least let him not be killed.*

That, too, seemed a fragile hope, and she felt the warm trickle of tears as her eyes betrayed her in her determination to conceal her longing dreams.

Chapter Ten

The mule lifted its head and watched as the two humans came down the winding path to the pond, the man hobbling badly. "Blinky," as Melody had christened the lop-eared mule, was puzzled. He had never seen the two humans together before. Not in his own realm, that of the pond, its surrounding willow and cattails, buffalo grass, deer, quail and meadowlarks. The man's face was set grimly. The woman carried a sack slung over her shoulder. With her free hand she held the limping man's elbow. This was going to be a rare day, Blinky decided, and he doubted that he would enjoy it.

They rode westward at the mule's regular plodding pace. Melody controlled it with a hackamore she had devised and Featherskill rode behind her, shifting uncomfortably as he tried to find a position which did not hurt. How long had he ridden hurt and awakened stiff and sore? Maybe Melody was right, everyone was right—it was time to settle down.

The day had begun brilliant and cool. To the north

there were storm clouds hovering on the horizon, however. Great stacked clouds which pulsed and throbbed.
They followed the wagon tacks westward, crossing the
long endless plains.

"These wagon tracks have been cut recently," Melody
said across her shoulder. "They can't be the ones you're
looking for."

"No." Featherskill pointed out that he was not looking
for these tracks, but for any that might have veered off the
main course.

Around them small hills began to emerge from the constant flatness of the prairie, and ahead was a sawtooth
range and a rising plateau. Still miles ahead were the
bulking thrust of the Rockies, and once from atop a knoll
where they rested, Featherskill thought he had a glimpse
of a pair of snow-capped peaks.

By late afternoon as the mule walked on, the darkness
grew and the clouds closed out the sunlight. Sometime
near dusk the storm cut loose. Two strips of jagged lightning creased the darkening skies, then thunder boomed
near at hand and heavy rain fell, driving at first, settling
then into a low disheartening downpour.

Melody's short black hair was plastered to her skull
like a dark helmet. Featherskill shivered with the cold,
and he could feel Melody trembling as he held his arms
around her. The mule, rain-glossed, continued undisturbed along its way. When darkness fell they would be in
a fix. Their only choice would be to camp out in the night
rain, unclad for the weather, without shelter. Featherskill
continued to sweep the country, searching for some sort
of cover.

He once thought he saw a twinkle of light, faint and
dull, in the distance, and his hopes rose. It could have

been a wagon train, halted because of the storm. They could offer some sort of shelter, even if it came to sleeping under a wagon on groundsheets. But the light was swallowed up by the storm and did not reappear. Perhaps, he thought, it was for the best. They couldn't know whose wagons they might be. They could not even tell that the sun had gone down except the world became even darker. Clouds scudded past them, racing across the earth and the wind twisted and gamboled around them. Melody said not a word of protest, nor did the mule falter. It was Featherskill who had had enough. His leg and shoulder were screaming out for relief, but he stilled the impulse to call a halt to it—they still had not even the most rudimentary shelter and a night on the plains in these conditions would be beyond misery.

"Dan!"

Featherskill lifted his eyes. Melody, her clothes buffeted by the wind, sat straight on the mule's back, pointing into the near distance, and Featherskill could see them too.

"Lights. Must be some sort of trading post, maybe a small town," he said. "Don't lose sight of it." Even as he spoke, the clouds, dark and near, folded around them, shutting out the distant lantern light, but the mule continued on its way, following its instincts and within another fifteen minutes they saw the lights again, much nearer, and the small ramshackle village standing desolate on the prairie.

They came down out of the low hills to emerge on a straight muddy street, the town's main artery, it seemed. It led past a row of four buildings to a central area where a dozen other structures, most of unbarked logs, clustered together for survival against the wilderness.

"Pull up here," Featherskill said suddenly.

He did not know the town, could not see a sign, but the two-story building they had paused in front of smelled of horse and hay and there was a glow in its single window. "Stay up there until I see who's inside," Featherskill told Melody, who nodded. The iron-gray rain still poured, but the girl managed a smile of relief. The mud on the mule was hock-deep, and when Featherskill finally slid from the animal's back, he sunk into the goo four or five inches.

He waded through the mud to the door of the stable. The door stood open and Featherskill stepped in. "Anybody here?"

After a moment a gravelly voice called from the hayloft. "Up here. Be right down. Didn't expect nobody to be around on a night like this."

"It wasn't by choice," Featherskill said as the lumpy stablehand wearing a red-checked shirt, leather jacket and baggy jeans came down the ladder to dust off his hands and face him.

"Topper Simes," the doughy man said, sticking out a pudgy hand for Featherskill to shake. "What can I do for you?"

Melody had seen that one of the large stable doors was open and she had slipped down to lead Blinky into the rough building. "Got a mule that needs tending," Featherskill said.

Simes studied the saddleless mule, the youngster in oversized, torn clothing and nodded, saying nothing. Possibly he had seen worse-off refugees stagger in from the rough country.

"Is there any place we can put up for the night?" Featherskill asked hopefully.

"We got what Mrs. Dundee calls a hotel," Simes said with

a toothless smile. "A row of cots in the lobby, as she refers to it—two upstairs rooms with doors. She'll have space. Especially if you can afford the deluxe accommodations."

Having brought up the matter of money, Simes, who held the lop-eared mule by his roughly made halter, looked inquiringly at the two strangers: The tall crudely shaven man with the bandage on his shoulder and a sawed-off pantleg, the younger fellow with trousers four sizes too big and raggedy old shirt with the sleeves missing.

"Just a minute," Featherskill said. He removed his right boot and took his hunting knife from his belt sheath. Then as the stableman and Melody watched, he slit the inner lining of his boot away, turned it upside down and shook out five double eagles. Simes smiled in pleased surprise; Melody cocked her head in admiration.

"I don't have no change for a twenty dollar piece here tonight," Simes said, "but I'll trust you for it."

"I thank you," Featherskill said, pocketing the coins he had hidden in his boot after Lovelace and Werth had paid him. He had given a bootmaker fifty cents to sew the coins in the lining back at Fort Riley. It was a safe little purse to carry along. And a man doesn't like to be stuck anywhere without some tuck-away money.

"Where'd you say this hotel was?" he asked, looking out at the sheeting rain. It danced silver and black in the feeble glow of the stable lantern. Distantly, they heard thunder rumble once more. It was going to be a long cold night out there.

"Sarah's . . . Mrs. Dundee's place is the third building down. This side of the street. You'll see it. It's the only white-washed place around."

"We thank you, Mr. Simes," Featherskill told the man. "If—" He peered into the darkness of the stable, took half a step forward, paused for a second look, and then just walked away from the conversation.

"What is it, Dan?" Melody asked, but he did not answer immediately. His eyes were fixed, locked onto the apparition standing in the far stall of the stable. The little paint pony looked up at him with a hint of recognition in its dark eyes.

"It can't be." But it was. The old paint he had purchased in Fort Riley, the one Ruthanne McGee had been riding when she disappeared stood there three-legged, watching the curious people gather around her stall. Running his hand along the paint's flank, he examined the brand, although it was unnecessary—he knew his horse well.

"Where's the lady who was riding this horse?" Featherskill demanded.

Simes flinched a little at the sharp tone of the words. "There wasn't no lady," the stablehand said. "Reggie Fortner found him wandering out near his place. He's been riding it for a week or two."

"Where's this Fortner now?" Featherskill asked fiercely. Melody clutched his arm, not wanting him to lose his temper, not understanding why he was angry. It had something to do with the raid on the wagon train, that was all she could be sure of. Nothing else could make him so mad.

"I can't honestly say," Simes said, calmer now. "Old Reg he likes the cards and his liquor. When he has a few coins to rub together he comes to town and—well, he plays the night away. You'll never find him this time of night, mister."

"If he does show up," Featherskill told Simes, "tell him I want to talk to him. Tell him there might be something in it for him."

"Sure, mister. I'll tell him. Is something wrong; is the horse stolen?"

"Yes, as a matter of fact. He belongs to me. But I don't think Reg Fortner stole it. I just want to ask him a couple of questions about how he came by the paint."

The rain drove down, obscuring the town, but Feather-skill and Melody managed to wade through the mud and runoff water, finding the porch of the hotel. It had no sign either. But they saw a thin severe woman in black standing behind a rough counter inside and a row of cots against the back wall. They went in.

"We need two beds," Featherskill said to the woman.

"Cots?" Mrs. Dundee asked in a nasal voice.

"We were told you have rooms upstairs."

"I do." She produced a book, dipped a pen in an inkwell and offered the pen to Featherskill, who somewhat illegibly wrote down "Hawkins and Carmody, Ft. Riley." Mrs. Dundee only glanced at the bandaged man's signature, and gave no attention at all to trying to guess whether the thin youth with Featherskill was male or female. Her attention was captured only by the twenty dollar gold piece Featherskill placed on the counter. Her manner immediately became more gracious.

"I'll have clean blankets sent up," she said, sliding the coin toward her cash box. She fished out his change in silver and smiled like a sick calf as he pocketed it and limped upstairs, supported by Melody.

"It's a room—I guess," Featherskill said as he opened the musty, dank little room at the head of the stairs.

"It's dry, Dan!" Melody said. She watched the storm rage on outside the window and Featherskill felt ashamed of himself for his complaint. Yes, it was dry, and there were two beds there. And how long had it been since Melody had had so much as a roof over her head, let alone a bed to sleep on? He sagged onto one of the beds, leaving the door open for whoever was coming with their blankets. Dull, smoky lantern light glowed in the hotel's interior, painting an oblong on the rough floor of the room.

"All right, Dan," Melody said, sitting on the opposite bed, hands clenched between her legs, "tell me about the paint pony."

And he did. Much of it she had heard before in their time in the cave, but parts of the tale remained mysterious to her. It was no wonder; Featherskill didn't understand it all himself.

"Then was Ruthanne kidnapped or not?"

"I don't know."

"If she was, why was the horse set free? Because someone might recognize it—anyone who had been traveling with the wagon train?"

"That could be it. I wonder if it had a saddle on it when Reg Fortner found it."

"You don't think he is one of the raiders?" They fell silent as a boy of twelve or so came in with their folded blankets in his arms, looked inquisitively at Melody and went away, leaving the door wide.

"Fortner? No, he's too much a local man from what we were told. The raiders don't stay in one spot—unless you count the town of Purdy, and since they're travelling west, they've deserted Purdy as well."

"What difference does it make if the paint had a saddle or not?" Melody asked. She tried to stifle a yawn, gave into it and gaped wide as she stretched her arms.

"I'm not sure," he admitted. "I have to talk to Fortner. I want to know if he saw any strangers in his area around the time he found the horse. If not, he still might have noticed some sign—footprints, a remnant of cloth. Something."

Melody had stretched out on her bed, tugging the blanket up under her chin against the chill of the night. Featherskill had risen to shut the door and leave the room in darkness, the rain streaking the window behind him.

"Footprints, huh," Melody said. "Small footprints, do you mean?"

Startled, Featherskill turned toward her. "What are you a mind reader?" Melody laughed softly.

"No, Dan Featherskill. I've been living with you for the past weeks if you don't recall. You talked a lot to me about your worries and I know that thoughts of the little girl, Beth, are not far from you mind."

He sat on his bed and tugged at his boots. "Well, she has to be considered."

Melody had her hands behind her head. She was looking at the ceiling, but it was as if her eyes were boring into his skull. "Don't tell me that, Dan. I know you too well now. When you were first wounded, you talked a lot in your sleep too. You'd be surprised at some of the things I heard. You may fool everyone else in the world with your tough, indifferent attitude, but I know better. The little girl was a big part of the reason you went along with Werth and Lovelace in the first place. She is more important to you than anyone, even Chalma."

Featherskill started to give her a rough answer, but her eyes had closed and besides . . . he didn't ever want to have to lie to this young woman as he so frequently lied to himself. Let Chalma escape, let him live.

So long as little Beth Lovelace was also alive and safe.

Morning was drab, the skies leaden and low. Occasional flurries of rain spattered the window and the wind creaked and fussed in the eaves and chinks of the building. Featherskill was up first, and he stood at the window, thinking gloomy thoughts. When Melody awoke and stretched she seemed to bring joy back into the day. Her smile was brief but wide. She shook her tousled hair and placed her bare feet on the floor.

"Morning, Dan."

"We've got to get you some clothes."

"I thought you wanted to find Reg Fortner."

"First things first. We eat and find some decent clothes for you. From what Topper Simes told us about Fortner's habits he won't be an early rising man anyway."

"I'm willing," Melody said, getting to her feet in one easy, catlike motion. Sadly, she studied her clothing. It looked much worse now that they had made town than it had in the wilderness where above all else it had been simple necessity. "Can you afford it, Dan?"

"We've got ninety-eight dollars left, Melody. We're running in good shape."

"All right," she said running her fingers through her dark hair. "I wonder . . . do you think it's possible to get a hot bath in this hotel?"

"We'll ask on our way out. One thing at a time, as I said. Food. Clothing. Then if they can manage it, you can have yourself a long bath while I try to find Fortner. Good enough plan?"

"It's a great plan!" she said enthusiastically. It had been three months since her last hot bath. It would be like slipping into a warm dream.

She found no little satisfaction in one other small, seemingly unimportant matter. When Featherskill had spoken about the money, she noticed, he had used the plural. *We've* got ninety-eight dollars left. Well, well, she thought with a smile, did that mean anything?

Could she begin to hope that it did mean they were becoming a plural entity? A foolish thought, perhaps. Melody did not want to engage in girlish fantasies. Still, she glanced at his strong profile, his thoughtful eyes as he gazed out the rain-glazed window into the obscured distances.

Still, one never knew, did one?

"Ready?" he asked, holding out his elbow to her, and Melody nodded, taking his arm as they went out and down the stairs. They paused long enough to ask Mrs. Dundee if she could arrange a bathtub in their room. She immediately told one of her young male helpers—her sons?—to start boiling water. Mrs. Dundee had been dutifully impressed by Featherskill's gold if not his costume.

They ate breakfast in the small restaurant next to the hotel. Only wide enough for a single row of tables, the place was nearly deserted in this weather and at this time of the morning. Ignoring the strangely clothed customers, the waitress took their orders and Featherskill and Melody waited while sipping hot, rich coffee. Melody put four spoonfuls of sugar in her cup without apology. Featherskill understood. He had been living on the same diet as she had.

After ham and eggs, biscuits with melted butter, and cup after cup of coffee, they asked about and went to the dry goods store. The man there looked startled at their appearance. He peered at them through his thick spectacles, a feather duster twitching in his hand.

"The men's clothes are on that table in the back," he

told Featherskill when he was asked. Peering at Melody, he added, "and the boy's clothing is on the next."

Melody laughed, but agreed that the boy's section was where she was most likely to find good travelling cloaths that would fit her. Selecting an off-white shirt and a pair of blue jeans, she waited outside while Featherskill paid for their goods.

"I'm going over to the stable," he said when he emerged, wearing a new fawn-colored hat. "I can't miss this Reg Fortner if he happens to show up early. I can finish getting dressed over there. You go ahead and take your bath and change at the hotel."

Featherskill didn't see Simes when he got to the stable, but he was relieved to find that the paint pony still stood in its stall. He took the time to change his clothes—a difficult operation with his leg and shoulder being in the shape they were. Dressed in a new forest-green shirt and black jeans he felt like a different man. By the time he had his boots back on and had tossed his old clothes into a rubbish bin, Simes had returned with a bag of oats over his shoulder, whistling pleasantly.

"Morning, Mr. Featherskill," Simes said, unshouldering the bag. The horses began to stir, knowing that breakfast time was at hand. "Found Reg yet?"

"No. I was hoping he might be over here by now."

Simes shook his head. "Old Reg don't care too much for daylight," he said. He peered outside at the gloomy dampness. "If you can call this daylight. Miserable weather, ain't it?"

"Where would he be most likely?" Featherskill asked, strapping on his Colt. Simes eyed the sidearm warily. "I'm just finishing dressing. I've nothing against Reg Fortner."

"I was wonderin'," Simes replied. He rubbed his fleshy jowls and told him, "He's probably sleeping it off in the back room of the Red Rooster."

"That, I assume, is a saloon?"

"You assume right. If you can call a four-by-eight shack a saloon just because it's stocked with liquor."

The rain had briefly lessened. Sunlight formed a bright fan as it fell through a rift in the silver clouds. Drizzle dampened Featherskill's face and plastered his hair down as he crossed the muddy road and walked uptown toward the Red Rooster. The saloon was not open yet, but a man sweeping the place out directed Featherskill to a rear room.

It had to be reached by an alleyway. The room was little more than a shack that had been added on to the back of the building, given a tar-paper roof and a leather-hinged door. As Featherskill approached it he heard a little shriek and watched as a woman in a blue dress and high boots squeezed through the door, banged it shut, and rushed off, slipping and sliding in the mud. Something was thrown against the door from the inside, followed by a grumbled curse. Featherskill approached the door with some caution. Pausing before it, he called out.

"Fortner! Reg Fortner?"

"Go away!" a thick voice yelled.

"I need to see you."

After a long silence during which Featherskill heard squeaking and the shifting of weight on a bunk, Fortner replied, "Whoever you are, go away."

"My name's Featherskill. I need to talk to you about the paint horse you're riding. It's mine."

"The hell you say . . ." In a moment the door swung violently inward and Featherskill found himself facing a man of sloppy bulk with hair covering his loose chest and belly. Fortner's eyes were small, dark and somehow pathetic. His thin dark hair was uncombed, his hand unsteady as he eyed Featherskill.

"Fortner?"

"That's right." He turned away, reaching for a shirt that lay on the floor. Without turning, he buttoned up and asked, "What were you saying about the horse?"

"The paint. It's mine."

"Who says?" Fortner asked slyly. He tucked in his shirt and turned around. Featherskill saw the man's eyes drift to the rickety table near the head of the bed. The whiskey bottle standing there was empty. Fortner's mouth tightened unhappily.

"I say it," Dan told him, "and everyone who knows me will say it. How'd you come by that horse, Reg?"

"Bought it," he said sullenly, sagging onto the bunk. He glumly looked at the empty whiskey bottle again. His thick hands were clenched together between his thighs.

"No you didn't."

"Sure did!" Fortner's words had no force behind them. He was lying and both of them knew it.

"Mind telling me from whom? Have you a bill of sale?"

"You ever see a real bill of sale for a horse out here? I haven't. Who's got paper and pencil with them? Not me. Why when this dude sold me the horse . . ."

"What dude?"

"Didn't get his name."

"Look, Fortner, I didn't come here to make trouble for you." He leaned against the wall of the shed, crossing his arms. Fortner tried to keep his gaze steady, but his eyes were wandering almost uncontrollably and Featherskill knew why.

"Then what are you here for?" Fortner asked in a nearly melancholy voice.

"I want that paint pony back. He's not yours and you know it. Someone took him from me out on the trail. I want to find that person. Tell me how you came by that horse."

"What's in it for me?"

"I don't know—maybe a finder's fee would be fair. You did catch the paint, feed him and tend him. I'll give you a fair price for your time, a small reward."

"How small?"

"We'll get to that in a minute. First, tell me about finding the paint. I've got a feeling it's very important." Featherskill reached into his pockets and brought out a handful of silver dollars.

Reg Fortner took a deep slow breath, looked morosely again at the empty whiskey bottle, looked hard and long at the silver money and said, "Buy me a bottle and I'll tell you what you want to know—all of it."

Chapter Eleven

Reg Fortner looked no better than he had on Featherskill's arrival even though he had dampened his thin hair and combed it back. He was feeling better, however, and after he took yet another drink from the bottle of whiskey Featherskill had supplied, he leaned back on the bunk.

"I got a little parcel about five miles out of town. I got some chickens, a nanny goat and a few head of maverick steers. Nothin' much for a man to live for, enough to make him wonder what he was thinkin' in the first place, buying the land . . ." Fortner took another drink and shrugged off his personal problems. "But you was asking me about the paint pony.

"One morning I was up early. It was just dawn and the land was all red and cool. I had had my morning coffee and three quick shooters of sour mash. Feeling good, I saddled my sorrel pony and went out for a ride, looking over my estate, you might say," Fortner said with a grin.

"I come up over a little rise that fronts my creek and saw something beyond. Thought one of my steers was wandering, maybe, so I started my horse that way. Well, it turns out it was this paint pony, standing there with its head down, looking tuckered and worn down.

"It was all alone?"

"Wait a minute!" Fortner said with some new spunk. He tilted the bottle again and relaxed. "The pony was alone, yeah, but as I rode toward it I looked off to the east and I seen 'em."

"Who?"

"Who? I dunno. I wasn't going to call out. Whoever it was that had left me a horse had gone off. I wasn't about to ask them to think twice about it. Don't have many mornings with good fortune shining on me."

"What did they look like?"

Fortner's eyes went blank, as if he was looking inward, deep into his foggy skull. "They were standing by a buggy. I saw the two of them—didn't I tell you the sun had just risen? They were nothing but shadows at that distance."

"You weren't curious enough to go closer?"

"I told you—I wanted that horse they had so obligingly left behind. No, I didn't go closer. Just looked like two men standing close, talking. One was quite a bit taller than the other. Then, when they got ready to leave, I saw one of them reach out and help the other into the buggy. Well, I knew then that it was a man and a woman, though she was wearing trousers as well."

"You can't tell me any more about how they looked?"

"I told you, din' I! I didn't go near enough." The bulky man was thoughtful for a moment. "Only one of them was wearing a hat, though. You know, Featherskill . . ."—he paused uncertainly—"it does seem to me that the shorter of 'em had longish yellow hair."

Featherskill felt his heart skip once. Ruthanne—it had to be. Then who was the man with her, the man with a buggy? One more thought clutched at his heart, and he asked: "Was there anyone else? Was there maybe a small bundle they picked up and put in the buggy?" *A small bundle. A small person. Where was Beth Lovelace?*

"No, mister," Fortner said slowly, carefully. "Them two, that was all. I waited until they were beyond the horizon, then I gathered up the paint. Not far away I even found its saddle and bridle. I looked at the saddle skirts, but there wasn't no brand or name scratched on it. I went home, counting myself rich."

"That's all then," Featherskill said, feeling perplexed and unhappy.

"That's all. All right," he said, making a decision, "I might as well tell you this too—there was another man asking about the paint. He said he had tracked it a long way and wanted to know if I had seen it."

"And you lied?"

"You bet I lied! Lied through my teeth and the man went away."

"What did he look like, this man?"

"Old guy wearing buckskins. Old plainsman, you know."

"With long gray hair?"

"Yeah. Riding an Army bay that looked just about worn down itself."

Rory Pitt. Pitt had managed to track the paint all this way west. That was one thing about Pitt, he did stick to the trail once he started tracking. But that did nothing to solve the mystery. Straightening up, Featherskill reached into his pockets again.

"I'll be taking the paint, Fortner. You say that's not your

saddle and bridle? I'll need them too. I'll pay Simes, of course." He placed five dollars on the table. "I'll leave you this for later. I hope that's fair enough."

Fortner nodded heavily, his eyes fascinated by the bright silver, his hand comfortable around the neck of the whiskey bottle. "It's just another day, Featherskill. Some mornings I'm right lucky, most days not." He collected the silver money. "All in all, I've had a lot worse starts to a day."

Featherskill barely recognized Melody when he got back to the hotel room. Wearing a crisp ivory-colored blouse tucked into new blue jeans that fit her body closely, she had scrubbed the months of dust and grime off her face, washed and brushed her short dark hair and even pinned a tiny pink bow in it. Melody saw him glance at the bow and she patted it, laughing.

"It's what you might call an affectation," she said.

"It looks fine." It did; somehow that single small touch brought out the femininity of her. That and the way her new blouse, the proper size and cut, fit her slender figure.

"Well, it probably won't last long." Her eyes narrowed questioningly. "Did you find Fortner? Did you talk to him?"

"Yes. He didn't know much." He told her what Fortner had said and Melody listened intently, her blue eyes alert and concerned.

"Then we still don't know much, do we? Not what happened. Not what happened to . . . not where Beth is."

"No." Featherskill sat on the bed, looking up at her. He had made his decision and now he told her. "There's nothing to do but to follow them. If I can find the buggy tracks after the rain. It won't be easy, but the wheels will have cut deep. Anyway, it's all I can think to do."

"Maybe we can catch up with Rory. He was on their trail before the rain started. "If his horse was as weary as Fortner says, we might be able to make up ground on him.

"I'm going to start as soon as I sack up some food supplies. The paint should be well rested, though it's not a fast pony either."

"Blinky never gets tired," Melody said. She was folding her old clothes, her back to Featherskill. "He never expends enough energy to get tired!"

"Melody, I said I mean to get started on the trail. The best thing for you to do—"

"Is to come along," she said, turning, her old torn clothes clutched in her arms. "I wonder where I should toss these?"

"Melody, you've been deprived long enough."

"Yes. I'm getting used to it, Dan. Besides," she asked, smiling ruefully, "where would I go by myself? I have nowhere else."

He was wasting time arguing with her, and he knew it. Intellectually, he knew the woman should not be hitting the trail with him, but his heart wanted her at his side.

"All right," he said, giving in. "We'll see if Simes has another decent saddle horse he can sell us."

"Blinky will be fine for me. He knows me. I can handle him with the practice I've had."

"Blinky is slow as molasses. He's stubborn and old!"

"That mule saved both of our lives too! He is my friend, Dan. Remember—I do not leave friends behind."

"If you insist," he said between clenched teeth. He already knew that there was no way to talk her out of the idea. He wasn't going to try. Nor was he going to tell her just then how much he admired her for her courage and her loyalty. "Blinky it is."

"Thanks, Dan." Impetuously, she went to him, rose to tiptoes and kissed him. It was only the lightest of kisses, barely brushing his cheek, but both of them felt their faces flush. Featherskill turned away before she could notice.

"It's all right. We're going to need to stop at the store again and find us a couple of coats. It's cold and bound to get colder."

"There is just one more thing, Dan," Melody said with an impish smile. She was holding something behind her back, and now she produced a straight razor. "Please?"

He rubbed his stubble-thick face and grinned. "You're right. It's about time, isn't it?"

The storm appeared to be breaking as they rode out of the tiny town, Featherskill astride the familiar paint pony, Melody riding Blinky. The wind gusted fitfully, hurrying the clouds and flattening the long grass before them.

"Is this the way to Fortner's ranch?" Melody asked, lifting her voice so that he could hear her.

"It's the way he pointed out. We should find it soon."

"Dan, he said the buggy left going north. Where could they possibly be going in that direction?"

"They won't be heading north for long," Featherskill was convinced. "West, always west where the stolen goods are more profitable. Colorado, where the mining camps are springing up and mining towns with them."

Ruthanne and . . . whoever it was that was with her, would make their way to the north and then turn west again. They must know of a trail. The wagon train had been scheduled to follow the Arkansas River, and anyone trying to run the raiders down would be forced to try that route, far to the south.

Anyone who had been trying to follow Ruthanne after

all this time was meant to have found the paint pony deserted. Left unsaddled, turned loose at a nearby ranch. The trail would have dead-ended there for the searchers. For Featherskill as well, assuming they did not figure that he was dead already, killed in the raid. It was just chance that Fortner had seen two people leaving the scene in a buggy whose tracks no one could possibly have connected with the lost woman.

There would not be many still trying to find Ruthanne. The settlers, impoverished and discouraged, would have other things to see to than tracking a foolish girl farther out onto the plains. McGee would follow—if he was not the man with Ruthanne. He and possibly her father, if *he* was not in cahoots with the raiders himself. There were so many questions that it did no good to take them all on at once.

Find Ruthanne. Whatever her involvement, she had to be found. She would be certain to know what had happened to her little sister.

Rory Pitt would not be as easy to shake as other trackers. Pitt would continue—he had been hired as an outrider; he was a friend of McGee's. He had begun the job and he would finish it. Pitt had found the paint and he would have noticed the buggy tracks. He might have guessed that there was trickery afoot. Pitt was far ahead of them now, but that bay horse of his, strong as it was, had had no rest for weeks. It was doubtful that Pitt could continue long without stopping to rest the animal, to forage for food.

They were approaching the Fortner place from the south now. Featherskill saw the shanty set down in a teacup valley surrounded by a dozen live oak trees. A rooster crowed and a dog barked as they rode past, Featherskill searching the land for the spot where the paint had been cut loose.

"Wish you could talk," Featherskill muttered and Melody glanced at him. "The paint, I meant," Featherskill said sheepishly. He would have to break himself of the long-trail habit of talking to himself and his horse now that he had a companion.

A companion. He tasted the word and found that it had appeal. He grew momentarily angry with himself. This was no time to think of matters like that. But his eyes didn't stray far or long from the bright-eyed girl riding the lop-eared mule.

"It's been a long time, Dan," Melody said, searching the ground herself. "And the rain was a hard rain."

"I know," he said unhappily. Perhaps he was over-rating himself. He thought of himself as a decent tracker, but he was no Apache scout. They halted side by side between twin hills. The wind drifted the horse's mane and tail and toyed with Melody's dark hair where the little pink ribbon still perched.

"Of course they wouldn't be going up and over hills in a buggy," he commented. "So we stick to low ground, following the natural trails. Game, Indians, all people follow a natural line of travel, the easiest and most direct. We'll cut a zigzag course of search. Slowly."

There were always small signs left in passing, though they took extreme patience to uncover. Broken twigs—a wagon wheel would cut an easily recognizable trail through a brush row. A shod hoof would nick a stone, leaving a scar a different color than the rest of it. In the low spots there might have been standing water even before the rain, leaving mud at the crossings deep enough to take the imprint of a horse's passing.

He still had hopes hours later although they had found nothing as they worked their tedious way north. It was a buggy they were looking for after all, and the ruts a wagon cut even in dry earth were easier to follow than a single horse's trail. If a person was lucky.

If. It was nearly sunset and still they had found nothing when Featherskill noted a dark green line of willows and cottonwood trees ahead of them. That sort of growth usually indicated a watercourse. It would be a good campsite for the night—and if there was a creek running behind the screen of trees, it may even have been used for watering the team pulling the buggy. Therefore, some sign might have been left of their passing.

Or, Featherskill thought, glancing over to see Melody's expectant blue eyes on him, maybe he was just a crazy man. What was the point in chasing ghosts across the plains? The damage had already been done, Chalma and his raiders were far away. Was he going on just to prove something to Melody? Or perhaps to little Beth?

"What do you say?" he asked Melody, nodding toward the lowering sun which was partially hidden by thick clouds, coloring them burnt orange and smoky purple. "Time we made camp?"

"We won't be able to do much after dark," Melody was obliged to answer.

Without having accomplished anything productive, they made camp that night. His thoughts were angrier than he let on. He was upset with the day's progress. Had they overrun the tracks of the buggy? Missed whatever sign they might have hoped to find back down the trail? He even went as far in his brooding as to consider that Fortner had lied to him. But what would have been the point in that?

They made camp among the riverside trees, rolling up as the wind continued to dance and complain among the dark branches overhead. The paint was tethered nearby; they did not bother to tie up Blinky. Featherskill hadn't even been able to run the mule off. It was doubtful it would stray and Blinky had a distrust of ropes.

Featherskill slept soundly and woke with the light of first dawn. A bit of colored light touched the small creek and tinted it a pale red where the shadows did not shelter the water. By the time he had rinsed off and saddled the paint, Melody had boiled coffee for them.

The shadows were still long and cool when they started from the glade, splashing across the creek and through the woods on the far side. Ahead, as they emerged from the trees was more long prairie, but the land rose and fell and slanted this way and that now. Occasional oaks and scattered thickets of nopal cactus were strewn about.

"West," Melody said, and it was no question. "How far does west go, Dan? It seems we are riding forever, arriving nowhere."

"It won't be forever, I can promise you that," he said, glancing up from the shadow of his new Stetson. "The raiders aren't settlers bound for Oregon or California. They'll want to sell what they've taken before they have to deal with the mountains or the long deserts. These are thieves, not pioneers. And a thief only takes up that line of work because it is the easiest way he can think of to make a living. They'll rid themselves of the goods as soon as possible."

"What about Werth's townsite? What about the people who've bought lots there? What about . . ." Melody's voice broke off. She was about to go on until she reached her point about the suffering the raiders had caused to so many, but her voice caught and her eyes widened.

Even Blinky was startled and he backed away from the mounded figure they saw lying in the shallow gulch.

"Dan!"

"I see it," Featherskill said, swinging down from the paint. He drew his gun and let his eyes search the bottom of the brushy draw. There were flies gathered on the dead man and Featherskill held his breath as he approached and squeezed his eyes nearly shut as he toed the body over so that he could see the man's face. He thought he recognized it by the clothes, and as the round bloodless face turned toward the white sky, his guess was confirmed.

Melody remained seated stiffly on Blinky's back. Her expression was rigid—curious and fearful at once. She could see the man's features, but she had known no one from the wagon train.

"Who . . . ? Is it someone you know?"

"Yes." He put his pistol away. He stood with his hands on his hips wondering how he was going to bury Adam Werth's body.

Chapter Twelve

"I never met him, of course," Melody was saying as they rode from the arroyo, leaving the sad hump of sand covering Adam Werth's earthly remains behind, "but from what you've told me, I thought he was one of the main suspects. I mean, he had the most to gain by stealing the building supplies, didn't he?"

"Maybe. Maybe he got double-crossed. Maybe. You know, Melody, he was the one who actually had the most to *gain* by making sure the wagon train got through. After all, he was deeply invested in the Star Development plan. If the town was built, Star would have owned almost all of it, having bought up the land and supplied the materials. On the other hand, he would have been ruined back East if the raiders' plan to steal the goods failed. No, Melody, I guess he was just a little man with a grand plan in the West that was too big for him."

"I wonder why they killed him here. Now."

"Maybe he made a break for it. Maybe it was a double-cross. It doesn't matter anymore."

"No. Could you tell . . . how long ago it happened?"

"Not more than a day or so," Featherskill told her. "That means we're catching up much faster than I would have guessed."

"Because they're traveling with heavy wagons."

"Yes. And camping each night. It takes time to unhitch at night and break camp in the morning when you're traveling with teams and wagons. Probably, they're in no hurry now. No one is chasing them."

"No," Melody said uneasily. No one but them was chasing a band of raiders and its stolen booty.

They had dipped into another sandy wash where willow brush and sage flourished. The land was dry again, almost as if it had never rained, so quickly had the ground here soaked up the moisture. The only indication of the storm's passing was a pencil-thin rivulet left to flow along the gravel bottom. Featherskill saw them suddenly—the tracks of two horses and fresh tracks. He turned in the saddle to call out to Melody when the rifle shot rang out.

The bullet whipped through the tall brush not far from Featherskill's head and he heeled the paint pony roughly. It jumped forward into the screen of undergrowth as a second bullet cut brush near at hand. Featherskill looked for Melody, but could not see her. Blinky had backed away in fright and begun to lope off. Melody was not on the mule's back, nor was she out in the open.

She had made it to the brush at least. Good girl—stay there!

Featherskill slid from the paint's back and began working his way upstream. Keeping in sight the sandy bank where he had seen gunsmoke rising. He moved in a crouch, gun in his hand, cursing his leg which was no longer shot through with pain, but felt numb and slow. He lifted his head above the thicket of sumac and sage and drew a second shot from above.

Cursing, he threw himself back and to the ground. That bullet had come from a different rifle. There were two of them up on the bank across the creek then. Perhaps there were more—or more on the way. Featherskill moved for a few yards on his belly then got cautiously to hands and knees. When he drew no shot, he waited for a moment in a crouch, eyes alert for any changing shadow, any glint of sunlight on steel, and then crept forward again, more slowly this time, each step taken cautiously.

He had no chance at the snipers from down here, he knew. The only thing to do was to try for high ground. If he did not make it out of the creek bottom they would settle in to wait up there until he gave himself away. Then they would have him. And if Melody moved . . .

Featherskill gritted his teeth. He was going to have to cross the creek and try to clamber up the far bank. It was no more than ten feet or so up, but there was no way he could manage to get a grip on the sandy face of the bluff and keep his gun hand free.

He continued to creep along until he saw through the tangle of bush a sort of cut in the wall of the bluff, a tongue of earth and rubble that had collapsed and formed a narrow ramp upward. If he could get across the creek without getting killed there was a chance he could scramble up the ramp, over rocks and roots and achieve the top of the bank.

It was a slim chance, and that was all. But there was no other opportunity presenting itself, and in the back of his mind Featherskill knew that the shots could have summoned more men, many of them. He placed his hat aside, took three slow, calming breaths and then made a dash for it.

His first lunge toward the open ground beyond the brush nearly brought disaster. His right leg cramped up and his dash instantly became a clumsy uncoordinated run. Simultaneously three shots from the bluff to the south exploded into the earth nearby, sending up sprays of sand. There was no turning back now, and Featherskill hit the creek running. The water was shallow, but the rocks underneath were smooth and rounded and he slipped again.

Cursing his battered body, he charged on. There had been a time, not long past, when he would have moved like a shadow from the brush to the sandy ramp, leaping the stream. Now he just managed to reach the notch in the bluff as another bullet from above sang past him, striking the ground within inches of his trailing boot.

He stumbled up the ramp for a few yards then went to his belly. He stayed where he was, lifting his eyes and the muzzle of his Colt toward the rim of the bluff. Anyone careless enough to poke his head up there was going to get an unwanted surprise. But no one showed. Listening carefully, he could make out no sounds of movement, no clink of metal on metal, no mechanical click, no whisper of boot leather over earth. Taking a deep breath he moved up the ramp, crawling over loose rocks and a tangle of roots.

There were two of them, he recalled. One to the south, the one that had been firing. And another to his left, northward. He hadn't seen that man fire. Maybe he had figured out Featherskill's move and had hastened to the south to cover the ramp, and was waiting there now with his rifle at his shoulder.

Featherskill was at the very rim of the ramp now, and he lifted his eyes over the edge of the bluff. Nothing. No one. The slight breeze ruffled the dry chia plants growing there and lifted light sand a few inches from the ground. The breeze made small sounds as it drifted past, and there was an insect hum in the brush below along the creek. Nothing else.

Taking a chance, Featherskill grabbed sand and hoisted himself up and over, rolling as he achieved the level ground. It was a good thing that he had. The man with the Winchester fired at nearly point-blank range. The sniper had all the advantages, but he had fired too hastily, nullifying them. And the old premise that a handgun is better than a long rifle for close-range fighting proved true again. From one knee Featherskill thumbed back the hammer of his Colt twice, triggered off twice and the sniper was struck twice in the chest, jolted back to land flat on his back, flies instantly appearing to walk across his still-warm flesh.

Featherskill didn't notice them, nor remain where he was to congratulate himself. There was an oak tree standing not ten feet away, and he dashed for it as if he was a target, and he had judged right—he was in the second rifleman's sights. As he dove behind the gnarled broken trunk of the oak two rapid shots snapped a dry twig from the tree and gouged out a deep furrow of gray bark, spattering Featherskill's face with splinters.

He could not make out the marksman's position. He peered into the sunlit whiteness, seeing no moving shadow, no rising smoke. Another shot rang out and another, and Featherskill buried his face against the trunk of the twisted tree. There was one more shot and this one caught his attention in a different way. No bullet flew past or impacted the oak tree. And the rifle was of a different caliber. A different make. It had the rolling echo of a deep-throated buffalo gun. A .56 Spencer or a big Sharps, at a guess.

"Come on out Featherskill!" a voice called and Featherskill grinned. This was no challenge but an invitation, and he rose and stepped from behind the tree to see the lanky figure of Rory Pitt approaching. The old plainsman was reloading his .50 Sharps rifle. On the ground between the two of them, Featherskill saw the head of a man, a red scarf circling his neck, his rifle dropped from nerveless fingers.

"Damn, am I glad you aren't dead!" he said.

"Had I been, I reckon you'd have been joining me," Pitt said. He removed his torn hat and swiped at his long gray hair with his fingertips. He stood looking down at the dead man, grimacing.

"Anyone we know?"

"Friend of yours," Pitt replied. "It's Walt Sample. Let's check the other one, odds are it's Karl Chambers." Pitt snatched up the dead man's Winchester and tossed it to Featherskill.

"I think it is," he said as they started that way. "I got a glimpse of him. He was a bearded man."

"That score is settled then," Pitt said. The buckskin-clad scout appeared gaunt and weary. They found Chambers and relieved him of his weapons as well, seeing that he no longer had any use for them.

"Now if we can only find their horses!" Pitt said with feeling. "I hope the shooting didn't spook 'em. I've been walking forever, Dan."

"The bay went down?"

"He couldn't give me no more. He was a gallant little horse, but the pace got to him in the end."

"They'll have had horses. Let's find them quick. Those shots might be bringing others."

"Are you mounted?" Pitt asked.

"I've got the paint! I'll tell you about it later."

"Good. Then what we'll—" Pitt stopped in stride, turned and gawked, his mouth actually falling open— something Featherskill had never seen before. The man was not surprised; he was dumbfounded. Featherskill turned to look in the same direction.

"It's only Melody," he said with relief. She was astride the mule, leading the paint up out of the gully. On her head was Featherskill's Stetson. This she waved in the air, smiling widely. The little pink bow was still in her hair. Pitt was awestruck. A woman out here in this country. A good looking little thing too. Where could she have come from?

"I assume she's with you," Pitt managed to say.

"Yes. That's something else I'll have to tell you about out—once we get out of here."

"It's going to be an interesting conversation," the scout said dryly. "Most interesting."

They found only one of the snipers' horses, but one was all they needed. It should have come as no surprise, but it did. The horse they found tied in a thicket was Adam Werth's pretty little blue roan. Featherskill told Pitt about finding the murdered Werth.

"Too bad, I kinda liked the little man," Pitt said, stepping into leather. They crossed the ravine and headed west once more. Now the very crowns of the Rocky Mountains could be seen through the blue haze on the horizon, thrusting snow-capped peaks and bulky shoulders skyward. As they rode, Pitt told Featherskill what had happened to him since the night of the raid. Most of it Featherskill already knew or had guessed.

"When McGee raised the alarm about his wife being missing, naturally I started out to look for Ruthanne. Most of the men did the same. Just after sundown I heard the distant rifles and I knew the raiders had hit the camp. I swung back, but it was all over by the time I got there. The settlers were standing around thunderstruck by the quickness of it all. When their men got back they discussed chasing after the raiders, but these are sodbusters, not soldiers, and they didn't have the heart for it. Me, I hadn't a chance alone and I knew it. The people drifted away, wandering back toward Riley with their women and children.

"Come morning I got to thinking—you must have figured it the same way—and I wondered at the coincidence of Ruthanne going missing just then. I figured either she was lost, taken or crooked. I decided to find her whichever it was.

"She hadn't ridden far east, but had turned her pony, the paint, westward after a few miles. She met up with two men and then went on alone all the way to that little hard-luck ranch where you say the horse was found."

"Have you figured out where the buggy came from, who was driving it?"

"No. I don't even have a good guess. The buggy, of course, could have come from that ramshackle town where you discovered the paint."

"That seems likely."

"Anyway," Pitt said as they dipped down into a dry-grass hollow, "the bay hadn't been fed well or watered enough. I had rode it too hard, and it foundered. I'm not proud of it. When the horse went down I started walking. I saw those two hombres back there just waiting around, doing not much of anything. I figured they were waiting to make sure no one was following. I was waiting for a chance to snatch a horse from them when I saw you—I didn't know who it was at first—and they moved into position with their rifles."

"They must have been smiling when they saw who it was," Featherskill commented.

"Not at the end," Pitt said grimly. He glanced at the young girl, sitting erect on the flop-eared mule's back and asked, "Want to tell me now where you managed to collect the young lady?"

Briefly Featherskill did, but his mind was more on what lay ahead than what had already happened. If the raiders had left men behind to watch the backtrail it might mean the raiders didn't have the big lead Featherskill had figured they had. Traveling with those freight wagons was slow going. You can't hurry oxen.

"They won't keep on for much farther," Pitt said as if reading Featherskill's thoughts. "They won't be crossing any big rivers with those lumber wagons, the bricks and hardware. They won't be climbing into the Rocky Mountain foothills, not with those tired animals."

"What do you figure their plan is?"

"Same as it was all along," Pitt speculated. "Build a town."

Sure, Featherskill considered. Stop, start throwing a new town together. Any goods, stock, equipment the raiders didn't want or couldn't sell quickly could be stored in the town and sold piecemeal. A new town built at no cost, rich with other people's belongings.

"We'll find them, Rory."

"There's only two of us," Pitt cautioned, but Featherskill's eyes were hard, his expression grim.

"If there's only me I'll find them," he promised. He hesitated in the asking, but he had to know: "Rory, the little girl. Beth. Did you . . . ?"

"I haven't seen hide nor hair of the tyke. We got to assume she's with her father and Ruthanne."

"As if that is a good thing," Featherskill said harshly.

"It could be worse," Pitt had to say.

After riding in silence for a while with the only sounds the whisper of the horse's hooves in the grass and the murmur of the gusting breeze, the scout said, "That scheme of sending Ruthanne out alone on the plains to draw us away from the camp—Dan, Lovelace wouldn't have come up with that plan. No father would willingly send his daughter out alone into rough country. Certainly Tyler McGee wouldn't ask his new bride to ride out in the Kiowa night."

"No, I don't think so either," Featherskill agreed. The two men locked eyes briefly. "It sounds like someone else I know. He would come up with something like that."

"He would, the cunning dog," Pitt said. "It was Ramon Chalma came up with that idea. I wonder, Dan, is Chalma partial to buggies?"

"I wonder if—. Ramon was partial to Ruthanne? If so we might not be seeing Tyler McGee again."

It was something to ponder. Could Chalma have met Ruthanne somehow? In St. Joseph, where perhaps the raiders were already studying Star Development's shipping plans. Where Chambers and Sample had showed up out of nowhere to ask for employment. If so, what would be the point in inviting McGee along for the ride? Maybe, Featherskill considered, they just hadn't been able to persuade the impetuous young officer not to attach himself to the wagon train. But why would Ruthanne marry the man. Featherskill wasn't certain. He was beginning to understand the possible source of the friction between McGee and his new bride. It was possible she wanted nothing to do with him because she was in love with another man.

It was possible that she was already in love with the suave and handsome Ramon Chalma. Featherskill knew too well the effect the dark young man had on impressionable women. His mouth tightened as he remembered how Chalma had come between him and his own sister, Laura.

A thought struck him like lightning. It was incredible, but all logic seemed to support the wild premise.

"Rory," Featherskill said, slowing his horse a little, "I think Ruthanne is Ramon Chalma's wife."

It was a dry fireless camp the three travelers made that evening. There was good reason for that. Although the land was still and dark around them, in the far distance they could see three small lights blinking. They could only be campfires. They were not far behind the raiders at all. Pitt, Featherskill and Melody sat close together, talking. Melody had a blanket over her shoulders, and her bright eyes reflected starlight. She had listened as the men again discussed the still-confusing situation. Now she spoke up.

"If Ruthanne is on Chalma's side—I'll leave the question of whether they're lovers, wed or two greedy people brought together out here—why, Dan, would she have gone so far out of her way to convince you to join the wagon train?"

"The same reason John Lovelace did. Chalma knew I was at Fort Riley. He couldn't ride into town to have it out with me. They would have strung him up. But if he could lure me out onto the plains, well, he could finish up his business with me finally."

"If Dan had been in camp," Pitt pointed out, "he would likely have chased after Ruthanne as well. Then Chalma would have Dan alone in wild country, and him with twenty men at his side."

"That seems like a long way to go to commit murder," Melody said with a hint of horror on her voice.

"I don't think"—Dan said with certainty—"that there is any length to which Ramon Chalma would go not to murder me."

It was not a cheering thought to go to sleep with, but it was late and they would have to be up early, long before daylight, and so, hiding a yawn, Melody told them good night and rolled up in her blanket to go to sleep against the hard ground.

"Quite a young lady," Pitt said, nodding toward Melody. "A lot of women would be grumbling over having had no hot dinner, fuss about having no bed to sleep on."

"She's endured worse without complaint," Featherskill answered in a low voice. He looked at Melody's sleeping form himself. "But you're right, Rory. She is quite a young lady."

Chapter Thirteen

The buildings were much farther along than Pitt or Featherskill could have imagined. It was remarkable, really, they thought as they sat their ponies on the wooded hillrise watching the activity in the valley below.

"They'll have themselves a town in another week or so," Pitt said in amazement.

It was true. From their position among the jack pines and scattered cedar on the outcropping they could look across the five-mile-square valley and see almost directly below them where the northern river half-circled the building plots. Lumber had been thrown up, cross-bracing added, beams raised. Three of the eight buildings had the beginnings of roofs. The ringing echoes of hammers and the thin rasping sounds of sawing was continuous. Dozens of men worked below. A hod carrier wheeled a barrow full of white bricks along the roughly graded main street. Two men on ladders were attempting to raise a freshly painted sign on a building front.

"I'd never have believed it," Pitt said, shaking his head.

"The labor force must have been here and waiting, the lots already leveled," Featherskill said. The carpenters and masons they saw were obviously not raiders, but skilled craftsmen brought in from Pueblo or possibly Denver to erect the town.

"It took some planning," Pitt commented. "A lot of planning."

"Well, this was no sudden impulse, Rory. It was the plan all along—building a new town out here, bringing the supplies in. The men would have been hired well in advance."

"The town was supposed to be farther south, Dan. What do you think? That Star Development hired these men and paid for their labor and then Lovelace and Werth came up with their own idea—simply moved the town to a new site?"

"Likely. One or the other of them. Maybe both. Chalma would have located the townsite for them. It looks like they were all in on the plan from the start."

"Lovelace is going to be one wealthy man," Pitt said.

"No, he isn't. He's going to be one poorly fed, poorly dressed prisoner."

"How do you plan to cause that to happen, Dan?"

"That, my friend, is something we need to talk about quite seriously."

Having surveyed the townsite, going as near as they dared, they pulled back to where Melody waited at a small camp. They told her what they had found.

"Chalma will have men out patrolling the town, won't he?" she asked.

"Maybe. It could be that he counts this as a project completed. Leaving the town in Lovelace's hands, he might have moved on to bigger and better things."

"Like robbing a bank? Stealing a trail herd?"

"Anything at all that's profitable. I wouldn't pretend to outguess Ramon Chalma. I could be wrong, of course, as careful as we've been, there still could be men out riding the circuit."

"I think you were right the first time," Pitt said. He was squatted on his heels, his hat beside him on the ground. "No sense in wasting fighting men on a job like this. What would they have to fear anyway? They must think I've pulled off the trail; probably figure you for dead. Even if one of us did happen to show up, what would they have to worry about? One of us arresting the whole town? Turning the workers against Lovelace? He's the man who pays their wages."

"I hope there aren't lookouts posted, but we can't be sure. We'll assume there may be men out watching for us—after all, Chambers and Sample were back there waiting for us."

"True," Pitt said thoughtfully.

Melody had been watching them, her eyes going from one man to the other. "So what are we going to do?"

"That's something Rory and I still have to work out, though I have my ideas. *You,* Melody, have reached the fork in the road where you're going to have to separate from us. I won't have you involved in any gunplay. I still have some gold money left, and the ride to Pueblo is relatively safe and short from here. You can do as you wish once you reach it. Find a cottage, maybe and wait for us. Or, you can get a stage out of Pueblo up to Denver. You'd like it there; it's getting to be a real city."

Melody didn't answer. She didn't even look at Feather-skill. She went to the saddlebags Blinky had been carrying and removed some tinned goods which she started opening with a skinning knife.

"The woman didn't seem to hear you, Dan," Pitt said with the hint of a smile creasing his tanned, lined face.

"Oh, she heard me. Didn't you, Melody?"

Melody glanced at Dan, placed one tin of potted beef aside and reached for a second. Then she started to sing. Softly and cheerfully. Featherskill felt the hot blood rising in his face. He started to rise, started to say something, to yell. But . . .

"There just isn't much more you can say that she's going to listen to, Dan," Pitt said, getting to his feet, planting his hat and walking out into the cool shadows of the wind-shifted pines.

"Melody?"

"Yes, Dan?" Her sparkling eyes met his and her singing broke off as she watched him, waiting.

"Need any help with whatever that is you're fixing?" The other conversation was over, he knew. There was no way he could convince Melody, and he had no authority to order her away. He watched a squirrel travel up the limbs of a shaggy cedar, leaping from limb to limb, and he wondered if he was unhappy or quite pleased that she would not mind him.

Dusk was purpling the sky above the forested hills. A thread of orange limned the skyline. Distantly, the Rockies stood unchanging, undisturbed. Shadows collected and merged and the air began to grow chilly.

Featherskill told Pitt: "Let's go down and have our look."

To Melody he had again pled caution, but her answer was, "Look, Dan, I'll pull back farther into the forest. I've got a Colt, a long gun and Blinky. I'll be fine."

Featherskill and Pitt had decided to lead their horses along with them, although this would make them more visible. If a quick escape was required, they would need their ponies under them. Besides, as Featherskill had pointed out, this was a new town, not even built yet. Every man was a stranger here. The men would only know their fellow workers, perhaps a few acquaintances from the trail up, but no one had been around long enough to tell a potential troublemaker from a man with important business to be done.

Dan thought of himself as both.

They walked their ponies down the wooded slope and then across the flats to a back alley. The air was heavy with the scent of pines and cedars, with the smell of creosote and fresh-sawn lumber. The town was dark except that here and there lanterns hung from raw beams. Under these men clustered to gamble, talk, eat, and drink. What Featherskill and Pitt were looking for was the town's headquarters, the place where Lovelace or Chalma, McGee and Ruthanne would be staying while their new quarters were constructed.

Earlier Pitt had said, "Won't that be just grand for Lovelace? Living in fine rooms in a brand new hotel, maybe a big new house. Basking in easy luxury, respectability and wealth . . . all built on other men's bones and broken fortunes."

Featherskill hadn't replied at the time. There was nothing to be said to such statements. But Pitt was right, Lovelace and his loyal followers were no doubt just counting the days until such a vision became reality. The way the timbers were going up, it didn't seem like it would be long before he had his grand house. With the crew they had and all the materials needed already on the site, a town could go up practically overnight.

"Look," Pitt said, nudging Featherskill's shoulder, and he nodded. There was a low, long building with its walls already in place, although the doors had not yet been hung. A livery stable, Featherskill took it for. And it was usual out here in snow country to first build shelter for the animals.

His eyes swept the dark streets as they moved through the skeletons of rising buildings. He was looking for trail horses, for roughly dressed men with belt guns or rifles in hand. Was it a good guess that Chalma and his raiders had moved on, having no interest in the actual construction of the town? Or was it just luck that Featherskill and Pitt had not yet run into them?

The air was scented with the smells of turned earth and kerosene smoke. From the highlands the scent of deep forest wafted. Featherskill and Pitt stood behind the stable in the deep shadows cast by the green-lumber building.

"You see 'em?" Pitt asked, indicating the two humped shapes across the clearing beyond where a stack of lumber had been piled. Featherskill nodded. Up against the oaks growing there were two covered wagons. One of them had a low-burning lamp showing through the canvas wall.

"Which one do you like?" Featherskill asked in a whisper.

Pitt nodded at the nearer one, the one with the lamp burning. "I always prefer to do my hunting in the light," he said.

Ground-hitching their ponies, they crept across the open yard, first darting to the pile of new lumber where they waited, hearts racing, and again let their eyes search the area. No guard could be seen. They probably figured there was no need for one, not in the heart of the new town with workers all around.

"Let's have a look," Featherskill said. They moved out of their place of concealment toward the silent wagon. Nightbirds chittered in the oaks and from far behind them a man roared with laughter at an unheard joke.

The tailgate of the wagon was down. Peering in, Featherskill saw the man jump, reaching for a pistol lying on a nearby trunk. But Featherskill had already made his move, throwing his leg up over the wagon's tail gate, and he had Tyler McGee in his sights before the young man could retrieve his gun.

McGee's hands went up, and the ex-soldier, dressed in trousers and a long john shirt, suspenders hanging, backed away. Ruthanne, wearing her petticoats, sat in front of a small oval mirror, her hair down, a brush in her hand, her expression that of a cornered adder. Featherskill heard Pitt slip into the wagon behind him.

"Make a sound and I'll club you down," Featherskill growled. He was hot and angry. The man had turned traitor and caused the deaths of innocent settlers. Featherskill turned his eyes to the blond woman. "That includes you, lady."

"You know my name," she said coldly.

"I wish I didn't. I wish I had never met you. Where's Beth?"

"You don't need to know." Ruthanne smiled infuriatingly and carefully placed her brush down. Featherskill watched her hand carefully. He wouldn't put it past her to have a gun tucked near at hand, not considering what he now knew of her. Those blue eyes, formerly so honest and innocent appearing, now glittered like glittered like snake's.

"Why'd you do it, Tyler?" Pitt asked. The hurt and disappointment he felt in his friend were obvious.

"I didn't set out to . . ." McGee stammered and halted. He had no good answer, and he knew it.

"Love?" Pitt persisted, looking at Ruthanne with hard eyes.

"Yes, Rory!" the former lieutenant said with something close to relief. "I can't deny my wife anything. It's a fatal weakness." His eyes were pleading, his face sagging. Featherskill was having none of it.

"She's not your wife, Tyler," Featherskill told him with hard, staccato words. "Never could be. You're a complete fool."

"You're crazy! She's my wife. You were there, Pitt. You saw the preacher tie the knot."

Pitt didn't answer. The scout stood at the rear of the wagon, gun leveled, his eyes going now and then to the yard outside, watching for intruders. Featherskill had to say it.

"She's married to Ramon Chalma. Or she thinks she is," Featherskill said calmly, watching Ruthanne's expression change from hate to pride to anger.

"I am, so what!" she said standing. McGee looked as if he had been shot. His expression was one of sheer horror.

"You don't know what you're saying, Ruthanne," McGee said.

"I do. I should know who I'm married to, shouldn't I?"

"You should," Featherskill said carefully. "I'm no lawyer, but I expect that it's Tyler here. You see, Ramon Chalma couldn't have married you legally. He's already married, Ruthanne—to my sister, as a matter of fact."

"You're crazy!" she faced Featherskill with her small fists clenched furiously. "He wouldn't—"

"Chalma wouldn't?" Featherskill asked, expecting no answer. "Of course he would. He'd do anything that happened to suit him at the moment. You don't know Chalma—I do. Too well. You're fools and dupes, the both of you."

"Where is Chalma?" Pitt wanted to know.

"I won't tell you," Ruthanne said defiantly. "You're liars anyway."

"She doesn't know," McGee said, lowering one hand to run it through his copper-colored hair. He was a shattered man. Perhaps he had long since begun to suspect the truth and they had only confirmed it. "He wouldn't tell her. I heard them talking."

"Who killed Adam Werth?" Featherskill wanted to know.

"He's dead?" Ruthanne said, genuinely startled. "Ramon said they wouldn't—"

"Ramon says a lot of things," Featherskill replied. "I asked you before—where's Beth?"

"I won't tell you!"

"No one told me," McGee answered, a man bewildered. "Is she gone?"

Featherskill had taken two quick steps forward to snatch up the revolver McGee had been reaching for. The former officer paid no attention to the action. "Got any rope around?" Featherskill asked.

"What for . . . you don't mean?" McGee was in a blind panic now. He looked to Pitt for comfort. "You wouldn't take me in, Rory? After all the times we had. I saved your life once, remember?"

"Too well," the old scout answered. "But you've been the cause of other men dying. The scales have come unbalanced, Tyler. We're taking you in. Ruthanne too." He looked at Featherskill who nodded agreement.

"You're wasting your time," Ruthanne spat. "You'll never get us out of town. If you do, do you really think that you can outrun Ramon Chalma across the plains? All the way to St. Joseph, Fort Riley—wherever it is you mean to take us?"

Featherskill spoke conversationally to Pitt, ignoring Ruthanne's outburst. "I think Pueblo. It's a lot closer, and we can stay in forested country for much of the way."

"He'll find you! He'll kill you!" Ruthanne shouted.

"I hope he does find me. As to killing me, well, we shall see. He's had his try before this and I'm still alive. Now, Ruthanne, you can either shut up or have a gag stuffed into your mouth. Which will it be?"

"She can't be quiet," Pitt said. "No sense giving her a choice. I'll gag her."

"You wouldn't dare!" Ruthanne said defiantly. But Pitt did dare, and within minutes the woman was bound with a strip torn from her own petticoat. While he was at it, Pitt said, "Don't bother with finding a rope, Dan. This will do fine," and he tore several more long strips from Ruthanne's petticoat as she twisted and struggled angrily.

"What now?" McGee asked defeatedly as Pitt bound his wrists behind his back and began to gag him.

"Now we arrest Lovelace. Is he in the other wagon?" McGee nodded mutely as Pitt tightened the gag in his mouth. "Alone?" Another nod, and Featherskill said, "Good. I don't want this to be any harder than it has to be."

Featherskill took a look outside the wagon and told Pitt, "Get Tyler here to show you where their horses are. Then start back toward camp."

"And you?" Pitt asked with some concern.

"I'm going to deliver a message to Mr. John Lovelace. If he's sensible about things, I'll meet you back at camp. If you hear shooting, drag it for Pueblo. Get Melody out of here."

Ruthanne was trying to scream something, to curse maybe. The sounds were pleasingly muffled and Feather-skill smiled savagely at her and said, "I'll try to bring Ramon in alive so the two of you can hang together."

He and Pitt got the two prisoners out of the wagon. The yard remained silent. The workers beyond had begun to put out their lamps and roll up to sleep. Tomorrow was a working day for them. Pitt had short leads on the bound wrists of his two captives and he urged them across the yard at the point of his pistol. Ruthanne struggled, trying to wriggle free. McGee was a broken man, he went along without protest. Featherskill waited until they were lost in shadows. He saw moonlight pick out the blue roan's flank as it was walked from the yard, and then he saw no more. He crossed the space between the two covered wagons in silence as the darkness grew deeper.

His night's work had only begun.

Chapter Fourteen

Featherskill eased toward the sleeping wagon, moving through the deep shadows cast by the surrounding forest. The men at the townsite were mostly silent now, and there was no stirring in the forest beyond. Pistol held loosely at his side, Featherskill reached the tailgate of Lovelace's covered wagon and held his breath, listening.

"Come on up, Featherskill," Lovelace's raspy whisper said. "I've been expecting you." Featherskill held still, not daring to make a move. "I don't have a weapon, Featherskill. At least not to use on you."

Not completely taking Lovelace at his word, but reading the weary surrender in the wagon master's voice, Featherskill risked it. He slipped onto the tailgate and entered the wagon. By the faint light of the descending moon, he could see Lovelace, haggard and weary, sitting on a chest dressed in his nightshirt. He lifted bleak eyes to Featherskill.

"I expected you," Lovelace said, containing his booming voice.

"You'd better get dressed. Where's Beth?"

"Right here," Lovelace said, getting to his feet. Peering into the darkness of the wagon then, Featherskill could see the little girl asleep on a bed of ticking, a blanket pulled up to her nose. Her golden curls spilled out across the blanket. Her breathing was soft and easy.

"I guess you're wondering . . ." Lovelace said, pulling his nightshirt over his head and tossing it aside.

"I'm wondering about a lot of things," Featherskill answered. He sat on a crate near the tailgate, Colt on his lap, his eyes shifting from Lovelace to the open yard outside. "But you don't have to tell me. There'll be a judge who's just as interested as I am. He'll listen to anything you have to say."

"I want to tell you," Lovelace said, buttoning a red shirt as he spoke. "I never thought I could come to this. Greed, it was—and laziness. I wanted my daughters to have everything I never had. I was beat, worn out, Featherskill. My life on the plains had beaten me up. When Adam Werth approached me, I took him up on it."

"So Werth was in on it too?"

"Yes. He was the one Chalma had contacted first. Werth must have thought it an easy way to gain his own financial independence. After all, Chalma didn't want the building materials. Had no use for them, living as he does."

"And you just decided to go along with them?"

Lovelace frowned, tucking in his shirt. "You know, Featherskill, it wasn't that easy. I tried to back out. Not openly! No, I really did try to convince Colonel Sheen to send troops along with us, knowing Chalma wouldn't dare attack an Army escort, but as you know I failed to make my case."

"So you just went along with the scheme?"

"I wasn't going to cross Chalma," Lovelace said with a sort of horror. "I'm not that much of a man, Featherskill. That's what happened to Werth. He proposed a new way of splitting the profits to Chalma, and—"

"I know what happened to Adam Werth, I buried him."

"Yes. There was that, and then Chalma did make other threats to me early on." He nodded at the sleeping child.

"He threatened to kill her?" Featherskill asked in astonishment. "I can't believe that even of Chalma."

"No, it was that he threatened to kill me. Where would that leave Beth?"

"I see what you mean, yes."

"Of course, Ruthanne had already fallen for the ruffian. They were secretly wed, did you know that?"

"I'd guessed it," Featherskill said without telling the wagon master about Laura.

Lovelace sighed and tugged his boots on. "I tried to keep that young fool, McGee, away from my daughter, but he was positively infatuated. I even allowed them to go through with a sham marriage." There was agony in his words.

"Otherwise you would have had to tell him about Chalma."

"Yes. Neither Ruthanne nor I could do that, of course! And so . . . and so, here we are." He stood, hat in his hand. "What are you going to do with us now, Featherskill?"

"It's called a citizen's arrest, Mr. Lovelace. I was hired to protect the settlers; I failed at that. Well, I still intend to look out for their interests. I'm taking you to Pueblo where you'll be jailed and either tried there or transported under Army guard to Fort Riley; that's the authorities' decision. I don't know what they will do, but that's what I am going to do."

"And Beth?" Lovelace nodded toward the sleeping child. "What will become of her now?"

Featherskill had no answer. It was a tormenting question. What would happen to the child? Her father had gone bad and that was all there was to it in the law's eyes. But what would Beth's eyes see?

Would she ever trustingly admire Featherskill again? He forced himself to put the consideration aside for the time being. They had to ride, to join the others at the high camp.

"Wake her, Lovelace. Dress her for traveling. It's cool in the mountains."

Lovelace went silently to his daughter's small bed and placed a gentle hand on her shoulder. Beth blinked and stretched all four limbs. Then she sat up; seeing that it was still dark her face grew perplexed. Then she caught sight of Featherskill and a small joyous sound passed her lips.

"Featherskill! You see, Daddy? I know you were worried. Now you don't have to worry anymore. Featherskill is here and if he has to, he'll kill a hundred bad men to keep us safe."

Lovelace glanced dismally at Featherskill and then gently dressed his young daughter, shushing her for everyone's protection. When she was dressed, bundled against the night chill, they slipped from the wagon. Featherskill picked up Beth and told Lovelace, "You'd better carry her. Where's your horse?"

"Too far. In the new stable, but I know where I can get another one." He nodded toward the oaks along the passing river. "There's some of the remuda picketed in the trees."

Featherskill eyed the man suspiciously, but Lovelace promised him, "There's no one around. I wouldn't endanger my daughter, Featherskill."

He led them on the short detour to collect the paint pony, which Lovelace seemed shocked to see again, and then they went into the oak grove where half a dozen spare horses had been tethered. It was no surprise to see a buggy hidden in the copse. Lovelace selected a stocky sorrel at random, and they mounted and rode silently to the high camp, cutting a wide half circle around the sleeping new town.

They reached the camp just as the moon was sinking beyond the horizon. By starlight Featherskill saw the two prisoners, McGee and Ruthanne, seated with their hands tied behind their backs, against a huge old pine log. Their gags had been removed. Melody leaped to her feet and rushed to Featherskill as he swung down stiffly from the paint. For a moment her arms raised, and she started to say something besides what she did say, "Welcome back, stranger. You had us a little worried." Then she saw Beth and she smiled, taking the girl from her father.

Pitt wandered over as Lovelace, untied, ungagged sat his horse before Featherskill invited him down. The old man looked like death; all of the heart was gone out of him.

"Made it, did you?" Pitt said.

"Looks like it. How about the prisoners? Give you any trouble?"

"What could they do? Ruthanne takes a yakking fit from time to time, warning us what's going to happen, but she runs out of breath quick."

"Ruthie!" little Beth said, pointing a chubby finger at her sister. "Why's Ruthie sitting like that?"

"She's been naughty," Melody said, not knowing how else to explain it to a little girl.

"Did you and she become friends?" Featherskill asked.

"Except that she hates you and I . . . don't," Melody replied, stumbling over her words.

Featherskill asked Pitt, "Think we ought to trail out tonight? All we've got is the stars to show us the way."

Pitt looked skyward. There were only the stars, but they were many and bright. "The timber's thin, Dan, and we should try to put as much backtrail between us and any trackers as possible."

"I think so too. Can we manage the three of them?"

"Lovelace doesn't look like he'll be much trouble, nor does Tyler. We can rope all three of their horses together, throw a loop around each saddlehorn. No one's going to run that way."

"All right. I think we're going to have to gag Ruthanne again, though." Ruthanne had started babbling on again, mostly about what Ramon Chalma was going to do to Featherskill for treating her like this.

"Ruthanne," Featherskill told her none-too-kindly, "I'd be surprised if Chalma bothered to come after you. Me—he might come after me because he hates me a lot more than he loves you. It might be worth it to him to have a chance at killing me. Beyond that—you'd better hope he doesn't come for your own benefit. You think things are dim right now? You have no idea what a life with Ramon would be like. If you do get 'rescued,' you'll live to curse the day he set you free."

"I don't have to listen to you!" Ruthanne hissed.

Pitt said as he bent over her, "No. And the same goes for us." He replaced her gag and after a few minutes' thrashing Ruthanne just sat glaring at them as they made preparations for the ride to Pueblo.

"What about the lieutenant?" Pitt asked.

"Tie his hands in front so he can ride. No need for a gag, I don't think. He won't be calling out to Ramon Chalma. I think Tyler understands the situation now."

McGee just nodded heavily, making no move as Pitt repositioned his bonds, except to stretch his arms to get the kinks out. They didn't even have to discuss tying Lovelace. There was no point in it. The life had seeped completely out of the man. He was not desperate or worried, just hollow and emotionless, a shell.

Melody saw the lack of light in Lovelace's eyes and to divert the child, she asked Beth cheerfully: "You ever ride a mule, Beth? It's so much more fun than a horse. If you like you can ride up with me!" The child's smile returned, and although she didn't comprehend what was happening around her, she seemed willing enough to ride with Melody on this great adventure of a trip.

They started out then, Pitt on the blue roan at the point, with the lead to a rope which passed back to McGee's saddlehorn and then to Ruthanne's. Lovelace followed expressionlessly, obediently. Then came Melody and little Beth on Blinky, and finally Featherskill, riding drag thirty or forty yards behind the body of the party.

The stars were clinging to a clear sky, and the pines spaced generously enough to make riding easy. But Pueblo was a long way off. And even after Pueblo, would Featherskill be safe? Not if he knew Chalma. It wasn't the prize Chalma would resent, but being beaten at his game. And by the one man in the world he truly hated. Oh, there were others Chalma would not hesitate to harm, to shoot down, but it was Featherskill alone who could inspire true hatred. It was Featherskill who had shown him up back in Clovis and run him out of the territory. Worse, everyone there knew that it had happened. Chalma had been humiliated. This episode would be seen by Chalma as yet another insult to his manhood.

Featherskill knew that and he was prepared for the end

of the game. There could be only one winner in the game and it could only end in one way—with one of them lying dead. Featherskill had avoided the end for a long while. Now he could not ignore it. He had provoked it and it would come. Sooner or later he or Chalma must die.

Dawn found them saddle-weary and hungry. There was no stopping, however. The land slowly brightened as the sun rose, the shadows stretching out from the trunks of the trees, the eastern sky coloring in a tangle of pastels: Orange, pink and lavender. The birds had begun to take wing and they saw a doe with twin spotted fawns grazing in the forest shadows.

"I don't like that much," Pitt said as they briefly halted at the forest verge to rest the horses and to study the land ahead of them. The wooded hills fell away, and the spread before them was rolling hills and flats dotted here and there with oaks and occasional jack pines. For the most part it was open country and would continue to be all the way to Pueblo unless they made a wide circuit, and Featherskill was not willing to do that.

"We have no choice, Rory," he replied firmly.

"Oh, I know that, Dan, but that doesn't mean I have to like it." Pitt smiled, but it was a grim smile. "What about the prisoners? They're slowing us down tied like they are."

It was a thought. Featherskill agreed. "Untie the horses from one another. I'll stay behind you. I don't think any of them will try to make a break—what's the point in it?—but I'll keep an eye on them."

"Are we going to camp?" Melody asked hopefully. She had walked Blinky to them. Beth Lovelace sat in front of Melody, but she was asleep. "Beth's exhausted."

"I know. We all are. I feel sorry for her, but we have to keep moving."

They started on again in the same file as before. Neither McGee nor Lovelace gave any indication of attempting escape. Ruthanne, on the other hand kept turning slightly in the saddle to watch Featherskill. Her eyes darted from point to point across the landscape as if wondering if her horse could outrun the paint given a good enough start. Featherskill rode with his rifle across the saddlebow, making sure she saw the display. He would never actually shoot her, but it was best to give her pause for consideration.

The sun rose higher, shrunk, and grew brighter. Featherskill tugged his hat lower. The sun was in their eyes now as they pushed on toward the horizon, yearning for the first sight of Pueblo. The ride was tiring, the constant vigilance it required, physically wearing.

The raiders came at noon.

Pitt looked over his shoulder toward Featherskill and pointed at the horizon. Dust could be seen drifting skyward there. Many horses, and moving fast. Featherskill looked right and then left. There was no shelter in the open valley. He motioned to Pitt to hold up. If they were going to be forced to engage in a gun battle, they would fire from the ground where their aim would be truer. The horses, Featherskill knew, were exhausted, too weary to attempt a dash for freedom.

He swung down from the paint pony as the first low silhouettes became visible to the south. Four men. Five. Six. Racing their horses northward. Featherskill gathered the prisoners and sat them down. Melody had slipped from Blinky's back, Becky in one arm, her Winchester in the other hand.

"Let us have guns, for God's sake," McGee pled.

"No." Featherskill's voice was iron-firm. Pitt looked a question at Featherskill. "No. He's changed sides once already, Rory."

Pitt had taken a kneeling position, carefully lining up his spare ammunition in ready reach. Melody, shuddering a little now, stood close to Featherskill, whose face was solidly set, lined with care.

"Give me a gun!" McGee begged again as the riders drew near enough so that they could see the color of their shirts, the lather on the hard-run horses.

Ruthanne's movement was so sudden that no one could have stopped her. She leaped up and grabbed Melody's rifle from her hands and swung the muzzle around, her eyes manic. John Lovelace leaped up from the ground shouting wildly.

"No, Ruthie!" And he lunged for the rifle. Reflexively Ruthanne pulled the trigger and they watched as Lovelace fell back, clutching his belly, his eyes astonished. Ruthanne went limp with shock. Featherskill grabbed the warm rifle barrel and wrenched it away from her.

Ruthanne gawked at her wounded father, frozen momentarily. Then she began to wave her hand wildly, screaming to the onrushing raiders.

"Ramon, Ramon!" she shouted, and the guns of the surprised horsemen opened up.

Featherskill grabbed Melody by the shoulder and swung her to the ground, firing three times with his Colt in the general direction of the riders, enough to breed some caution in them. From a prone position Pitt fired two aimed shots and Featherskill saw one of the raiders tumble from his horse's back. His boot slid through the stirrup iron and got entangled. His panicked mount fled from the noisy eruption and raced away, dragging the raider with him.

"Ramon!" Ruthanne screamed again, waving her hands in the air. It was the last word she ever spoke. From somewhere an aimed or inadvertent bullet impacted her chest and she staggered back three steps, eyes bewildered, shocked. Then she folded up and slumped to the ground.

Featherskill used his rifle now, firing seven shots as fast as he could work the lever. Pitt continued to shoot deliberately, confidently. Featherskill noticed there was blood on the plainsman's sleeve. Melody made some noise with her own rifle and they saw that the raider attack had thinned to three men. The onrushing force slowed, turned and split in confusion.

It was at that moment that Featherskill saw the fluttering guidon near the horizon and minutes later a troop of cavalry appeared, charging at the remnant of the force of raiders.

"Well, well," they heard Pitt mutter. "I knew there was a reason I paid my taxes."

Chapter Fifteen

The soldiers were out of Fort Lyon. It seemed that Ramon Chalma and some of his raiders had hit a few farms and villages down along the Cimarron, near the Texas line, and the troopers had been pursuing them for three days. Rory Pitt had served as a scout over at Lyon, so he did most of the talking to the officer in charge who knew him.

Featherskill was more concerned with other matters. Ruthanne had been shot dead by the raiders and McGee had at first set up a howl you could hear across the plains. Now he just sat near her shallow grave, rocking back and forth and moaning to himself.

John Lovelace had taken a bullet in the guts. He was not long for it, and he knew it. While Melody kept Beth occupied, Featherskill tried comforting Lovelace, but there was nothing he could do. The wagon master couldn't even drink water, it burned his guts so badly.

"I've had it, haven't I?" Lovelace asked Featherskill.

"Yes, you're a goner saving a miracle."

Lovelace's face was as dry and pale as a sheet of paper.

He held his stomach with both hands. Blood leaked through them.

"I sure muffed it," Lovelace said weakly. "My time on this earth." He didn't look at Featherskill, but toward Beth, who was playing some sort of skipping game with Melody.

"We all manage to make the wrong moves," Featherskill commented. It was of little satisfaction for Lovelace to ponder that.

"My Ruthie . . . she's dead, isn't she?" At Featherskill's nod a tear broke free of the old man's eye and snaked down his cheek. "My fault, Featherskill. I did that. Out of sheer greed. My other daughter, now." He looked again to where Beth jumped about innocently. "Now she'll have no family at all."

"We'll find her a good home," Featherskill promised, meaning it. Lovelace closed his eyes and then his bloody hand reached out and clasped Featherskill's wrist.

"That woman of yours . . . Beth likes her."

Featherskill didn't answer. It was true, but he didn't know what response he was supposed to make. "Ask her, Featherskill. Ask her if she'll take care of Beth for me."

"She's still a young woman, Lovelace. It isn't fair to burden her with a child when she has no people herself, no home."

The clawlike hand tightened on Featherskill's wrist. "Ask her! Ask her for me . . ."

Featherskill waited while Lovelace's hand fell away from his wrist, while the wagon master's breathing rattled shallowly and then stopped. The futility of it threw him into a dark mood. He rose on his stiff leg and snatched up a nearby blanket to cover Lovelace's face. He stood with his hands on his hips, looking across the empty land. Beth still played with Melody. A lone crow circled aimlessly in a clear sky. The soldiers had carted away the dead raiders and buried them. Here was one more job for them.

"None of the dead men was Chalma," Pitt said, coming up beside Featherskill. Then he saw Lovelace's covered face and shook his head heavily. "They say Ramon slipped away on the first night. Probably alone."

Featherskill just nodded. All of this had been so futile, bloody and unnecessary. Lovelace had had it right—it was greed that had caused it. Greed and a complete lack of concern for other people's lives. Featherskill himself just felt weary. His leg had not bothered him for a day or so; now it throbbed again, joining his aching head. His shoulder had stiffened on him. It felt locked up about half the time. What in hell was he doing out here? He pulled his hat down tighter and walked away from Pitt to talk to Melody.

Beth was collecting wildflowers under Melody's smiling eyes when Featherskill reached her. They stood silently watching the girl at play for a minute.

"I have to tell you something. Lovelace wanted you to take care of Beth."

"Of course," Melody said brightly. His eyes narrowed.

"You don't understand, Melody. He meant from now on. I wouldn't even have told you, but it was his dying request. How could I not?"

"It's all right, Dan," Melody said, placing one hand on his shoulder. "How could I not take care of her? She has no one else."

"Melody, do you have any idea what you'd be taking on?"

"Yes," she said, glancing at Beth who waved back, "a little girl."

He started to object, but Melody put a finger to his lips.

"Don't say anything. Beth is my friend, and you know how I feel about loyalty to my friends."

"You can't let loyalty structure your life."

"Dan—it's settled."

And it was. Featherskill tried a couple of more arguments, but by then Melody wasn't even listening to him. Finally he walked away. Finding Pitt near the cavalry camp, his wounded arm now in a sling, he asked the plainsman. "Who's in charge here?"

"Lieutenant Charles. That's him over there." Pitt inclined his head toward a young blond officer. "What do you want?"

"To talk to the prisoners."

"Not Tyler McGee?"

"No, the raiders." The two men walked to the officer in charge. Pitt told him along the way: "I guess the prisoners, McGee included, are going to be escorted back to Fort Riley for trial. I don't know for sure what they can charge Tyler with—except stupidity. The raiders will more than likely be fitted for hemp neckties. They won't find a sympathetic judge or jury at Riley."

"Ask if Beth and Melody can go along with them."

"I'm sure Lieutenant Charles won't leave them out here. Dan? You have something else in mind, haven't you?"

"That's right."

"Chalma?"

"How can this be finished if we don't get Chalma, Rory? He'll only gather another gang in time. He doesn't give up. He's found a sweet racket; he'll keep at it until he's captured or killed."

"It's too much, Dan. One man alone can't do the job."

"We won't know until I try," Featherskill answered, and Pitt could tell by the set of his jaw and the cold glimmer in his eyes that there was no point in trying to talk Featherskill out of it.

The lieutenant gave him permission to talk to the three captured raiders. They sat sullen and dirty in a group guarded by two armed troopers. Featherskill walked near to them and looked at each man's face. He knew none of them, but they were of a type. Tough, bearded, defiant.

"I want to find Chalma," Featherskill said, crouching down. "Anyone got any ideas?"

"He ran," a lean, man with one bad eye complained. "Our brave leader—he upped and ran when the Army came."

"Shut up, Campo," the man next to him commanded.

"Why? What's going to happen to me?"

"Chalma will—"

"Chalma won't do a thing. The Army's going to hang me! What can Chalma do after that? What do you want, mister?" he asked Featherskill.

"I want to find him and finish him."

"That's what he deserves, the sneaking coward."

"Any one of you know where he would have gone?" Featherskill asked, looking again at each of them in turn.

"Back to town," the third man, the one who had not spoken before, said from beneath the brim of a tugged-down hat. "He was going back to the town."

"You mean Purdy?"

"Naw, not that rathole! The new town, I mean. That's where he was going. Anything he's got left is up there. Men, horses, goods."

"I'll see if I can find him there." Featherskill rose from his crouch. The man called Campo growled.

"Do that. Find him and kill him, the coward."

The raider was wrong about Chalma, Featherskill thought as he walked away. Chalma was no coward. He had run when the troopers appeared not because he was afraid, but because he planned to live and fight another day. He left his men there to protect his back while he made his escape. Their fate did not concern him. In his mind Chalma was the center of the universe; only his own fate mattered.

Featherskill intended to make sure that fate was delivered to Chalma in a manner far outside of the framework of the raider's schemes. He paused to saddle the paint pony, to clean his weapons and check his ammunition supply. And then he was ready to pay his call.

Melody caught Featherskill before he left. He was already aboard the paint, and she had to catch the bridle to halt him. Looking up with those wide blue eyes, she said, "You were just going to leave without even telling me?"

"I thought it was probably better."

"It wasn't, Dan. You have some strange ideas at times. You thought that it was best for me to leave Beth with strangers. Now you think it is best to ride away from me—maybe for the last time—without a word? No, Dan, it was not for the best. Then I would never have had the chance to tell you."

"Tell me?"

"That I love you." She rushed on through his awkward pause. "I would argue with you, try to convince you not to go, it would all be useless, and so I won't. But you owed me the chance to at least have my say, Dan." Her hand fell away from the bridle.

He stared down at her for a long minute as the chill breeze drifted over him. The little pink bow, he noticed, was still pinned to her dark hair. He smiled at the sight. Yet he could not think of another word to say, not one, and so he turned the paint pony's head northward and started on his way, leaving the woman behind to watch after him.

The town had changed eerily since Featherskill had first seen it. It was empty, ghostly. The wind could be heard above the silence. No hammers fell, no saws rasped; there were no shouts from man to man on the building site. The town was as deserted as if a plague had swept through it.

No pay, Featherskill knew. For top wages the men would be more than willing to travel into the wilderness and construct a boomtown. But the wages were gone. Lovelace, the boss, had vanished with their pay. What was there to keep anyone in the town?

Clouds low, dark and menacing, gathered above the far peaks and the wind had a cold edge to it as Featherskill sat watching the ghost town from the pine ridge. The ghost of a town that had never even lived a single day. A monument to greed and slaughter. He started his horse slowly down the flank of the hill, moving carefully through the tall pines, the paint's hoofs making little sound over the pine-needle-littered forest trail.

The town had been deserted; it was only rolls of tarpaper, piles of brick, stacks of lumber. The skeletal framework of unfinished buildings—all deep in silence and cloud shadow. He flexed his right hand and touched his holster. He grimaced and swallowed a curse. If it came to a close-up gunfight, he had no chance. Chalma was cruel, violent, evil. But he was also a first-rate gunhand. Quick, accurate, deadly.

"I'm a fool for trying this," he told himself. He knew that even now Chalma could be in concealment, following his progress with the bead sight of his rifle, waiting for a clean, sure shot.

Reaching the spread of lots on the flats, he rode toward the side wall of the new stable. He swung down cautiously from the paint horse. He slipped his Winchester from its saddle scabbard and simply let the reins to the horse drop.

He removed his hat and placed it over the saddle horn. The breeze fingered his hair and pressed his shirt against his chest. He carefully levered a round into the rifle's chamber and left the hammer cocked.

Featherskill crept through the heart of what was to have been the town, moving as silently as the cloud shadows which had begun to stray overhead from the mountains. The silence was more than eerie—it was heavy with death, as if he was walking in a gravesite instead of a town. There was an open half-block ahead of him where lots had been marked out with pegs and twine. Featherskill hesitated before crossing the open ground.

Running in a crouch he made the cover of the next partially completed building. He smiled as he considered what a fool he was making of himself if the town was truly deserted. But he knew it was not. Somehow he could feel the presence of Chalma.

And so he was startled but not surprised when a shot from the roof of a building across the street slammed into the plank wall beside his head and tore splinters. Featherskill stepped ahead and rolled in through an unglazed window to land on a bare plank floor as two more shots sang past his head.

He grinned. It wasn't like Chalma, but the man had given himself away. He slid along the floor which was littered with sawdust and bent nails and lifted his eyes above the sill of the next window. He studied the building opposite. Perhaps it had been meant to become a saloon or a hotel. Two stories high, it only awaited the addition of doors and a false front before painting. From his angle Featherskill could see all of one of the flanking alleys, and the head of the other back for a distance of twenty-five feet or so.

Chalma, then, had remained at his chosen position. He was forted up and did not plan to come out. The silence held, except for the small scuttling sounds the wind made. The skies had darkened and the day had become damp shadows and dead empty earth. Featherskill did not move, did not call out a challenge. Let Chalma make the first move.

Chalma was as patient as he, however; both men had fought the Indians on various occasions and knew that he who moved first was likely the one to die. Featherskill's leg was stiffening up. His shoulder felt cold from lack of circulation.

He waited.

The only thing that would draw him out would be the arrival of darkness. Beyond that or . . . and then it began to rain. There had been no rumble of distant thunder to warn him. Lightning struck near at hand and the first thunderous explosion like a cannonade followed on its heels. The rain fell suddenly, and it was a hard, cold, driving rain.

Featherskill moved back to the first window and peered across the street. He could barely see the front of the hotel now through the steely mesh of the rain. A gusting wind rattled the timbers of the unfinished building and pawed coldly at his clothing.

Chalma would be coming. He was certain of that.

Chalma would use the storm as cover. He could not see the alleyways now or much of the street as the clouds, at roof height, swarmed relentlessly over the mountain town. He made up his mind to move.

He saw no back door, glancing in that direction, but it seemed there must at least be a window there, and so he moved that way, still in a crouch. Rain was falling through an unfinished portion of the roof and riveting off into the open, doorless cellar.

Featherskill stepped over the pit of the cellar and Chalma, his eyes wild, his hair in his eyes, his white teeth flashing wolfishly, appeared only a few feet away from him. The Colt in Chalma's hand erupted with flame and black powder smoke filled the room as Featherskill dropped into the cellar, landing roughly to lie limp and still as death against the packed earth floor.

An odd sound filled the building's dark depths, audible above the rush and swirl of the storm. A manic giggle issued from Chalma's lips. Featherskill heard it clearly, and then the steps of Chalma's boots nearing the cellar opening. He heard Chalma cock his pistol in the stillness. Saw a silhouetted form which was Chalma's head as he peered into the dark chamber where Featherskill lay. The silver conchoes on the choke collar Chalma always wore reflected light from distant lightning.

And Featherskill shot the outlaw dead.

His Colt was in his crippled right hand. Drawn silently, cocked and steady in his fist, he had waited as silently as death. Chalma had assumed he had made his killing shot, but Featherskill had been saved by a misstep into the mouth of the cellar. Chalma's shot had flown high and wide as Featherskill fell roughly to the floor below.

Chalma teetered, staggered forward a single step and

fell headfirst to the floor, landing on his head. His arm was flung across Featherskill. His Colt, cocked and ready to be fired again, lay inches from Chalma's dead fingers.

Featherskill wanted to lie there, to let his thoughts regroup, to wait for the pain in his body to subside, but having that stinking piece of meat on top of him was more than he could bear, and he flung Chalma aside, getting first to his knees and then rising slowly on wobbly legs.

Lightning crashed above them, nearer, and the cellar was illuminated briefly. By the brilliant light it was clear that Chalma was dead, that the long game was ended.

There was only one more thing to do.

Featherskill clambered clumsily up the temporary wooden ladder the workmen had left in the cellar and eased himself up onto the damp floor of the dark building. Beyond the windows the storm rampaged on. The world was dark, gloomy and wet.

He searched around a little and found what he wanted. In a rough storage room was the paint that would be used later to decorate the new structure. Among these cans was turpentine, brushes and rags. He pried open two cans of turpentine and poured the fluid generously over the rags, splashing the remainder on the wooden walls.

It only took one match to start the blaze.

The storage room went up in a muffled explosion as Featherskill backed away, shielding his face with his forearm. The new timber caught as readily as matchsticks, and within minutes flames were crawling across the ceiling, scorching the walls. Fiery tongues leaped through the open ceiling into the sky. The elements dueled: The rain driving down as the hot roiling flames met the storm's furious face and billows of black, acrid smoke swirled and rose to merge with the black clouds.

By the time he had gotten out of the building, the flames had already spread to the building next door. The wind was lifting embers from these two fires and drifting the sparks across the street. Those that survived the twisting rain found fresh fodder, and the flames grew, devouring the buildings on his side of the street hungrily.

Featherskill trudged through the rain and smoke toward the stable. The paint had had sense enough to enter the doorless stable to get out of the storm. Now he led the horse into the street and paused to watch the town burn. The flames were a glorious, gouting rush of destruction, burning furiously, undaunted by the rain.

By morning there would be nothing left of it, not an unburned beam, not a standing timber—only a sad, blackened futile collection of ash and a vague dark memory of greedy, ambitious dreams.

"Come on, paint," Featherskill said, turning the horse away from the destruction. The paint plodded down the muddy street toward the forest beyond. It was going to be a long, cold ride to Fort Riley, Featherskill reflected.

And then a short, pleasant ride back to his little upstate homestead with his new family in tow.